THE
TWILIGHT PRISONER

KATHERINE MARSH

DISNEP · HYPERION BOOKS
New York

First Edition

1 3 5 7 9 10 8 6 4 2

Printed in the United States of America

Library of Congress Cataloging-in-Publication Data on file.

ISBN 978-1-4231-0693-7

Reinforced binding

Book design by Ellice M. Lee

Visit www.hyperionbooksforchildren.com

To my beloved son
Aleksandr Edmund Barnes

TWILIGHT PRISONER

I | The Uninvited Guest

It was just before dusk in Central Park, and Jack Perdu knew he needed to make his move. Cora Flores, a fellow sophomore and Latin scholar at the George C. Chapman High School, sat propped against a tree trunk, blowing bubbles with her gum, and filling in the *New York Times* crossword puzzle.

Jack sat across from Cora, his skinny frame hunched over a copy of the *Metamorphoses*, his favorite book of ancient Greek myths. But the shrieks of children on the swing sets distracted him from his translation, and every few minutes, he stole glimpses at Cora. Even though she always complained about being fat, Jack thought she was perfect, without the bony elbows and pinched look that so many Chapman girls had, and with a wide, open face that made him feel at ease. He could tell when she was concentrating because she would forget to pop the bubble she just blew, letting it perch on her lips. It was a habit that got her into trouble during tests at school, where chewing gum was strictly prohibited.

With a loud pop, she burst a bubble and looked up. "Romantic poet who urned—spelled u-r-n-e-d—fame. Five letters."

It had been Cora's idea for the Latin Club to meet at the Arthur Ross Pinetum on this airless, Indian summer day. Ellen Davis, Cora's best friend, sat next to her on the grass, and at a picnic table nearby, two of the boys in their class, Gene Chen and Misha Zolotov, compared Latin translations. Above them, towering pines cast shadows over the swing sets and tables and the little dirt cul de sac called Contemplation Circle.

"Byron?" Ellen offered.

"No," said Jack, eagerly straightening up. "Keats. John Keats. He wrote 'Ode on a Grecian Urn.'"

Cora scribbled down the word "Keats" and smiled. "That's it! Thanks, Jack."

"No problem," he said. But he was secretly pleased that he could help her. Cora loved solving all sorts of puzzles—she was not only the best Latin student in the school but a natural at math and science, too.

"Hey, Ellen," said Misha, looking back over his shoulder. "We need your help with this translation."

Ellen closed her book and yawned. "Why don't you ask Cora or Jack?"

Gene flashed a shy grin. "Because we don't want the answer yet."

"Okay. Another lousy Latin scholar coming your way," Ellen said as she joined the boys at their table.

For a moment, Jack and Cora were alone. As he watched her absently tuck a lock of long, brown hair behind her ear, he tried out a sentence in his head: *So, want to get something to eat after we're done?* He felt his face turn red and looked over at the Great Lawn, the open green expanse just visible through the trees.

"I think you've got a sunburn, Jack," said Cora, pointing to his face.

"A sunburn?" he said, stupidly.

"Yeah, your cheeks are all red."

Now, he told himself. *Ask her now.* But instead he said, "It's warm out here."

"It's hot!" Cora replied, fanning her face with the crossword puzzle. "I can't believe it's October."

The words were simple: *What are you doing after this? Want to get something to eat?* He opened his mouth, trying to formulate the questions.

"That was a funny postcard you sent me this summer," he said instead. Over the summer, while he had been in Italy with his father on an archaeological dig, Cora had sent him postcards and letters, mostly about how bored she was in New York.

"Which one?"

"The one asking me if I had seen any sporting events at the Colosseum in Rome. You predicted that the lions would beat the Christians *clepsydra addita ad spatium mortis subitae.*"

Cora chuckled. "Yeah, in sudden-death overtime. Pretty good, right?"

Jack nodded. He looked over at Ellen, who was thankfully still arguing with Gene and Misha over their translation.

"Your letters were fun, too," Cora continued. "I liked the one about how . . ."

But Jack only half-listened. Instead he thought about the one letter he had written Cora but failed to send. It revealed his greatest secret—how last year he had been hit by a car and had started seeing ghosts. He had explained to her how one of them, a girl named Euri, had led him into the underworld beneath New York and helped him find his mother, who had died when he was six. The letter was the most honest he had ever written—except for one thing. He hadn't told her that he still saw ghosts. Every once in a while, always after sunset, he'd notice something strange—an old man reading the newspaper while floating six inches above a park bench, or a child chasing a firefly outside of his tenth-story bedroom window.

But since last spring, when he had glimpsed her in Central Park, Jack had never again spotted the one ghost he really wanted to see. He longed to find Euri and to tell her about all the ways his life had changed—he could talk to his father now and had a few friends—but, more importantly, about all the fears and doubts that remained the same. A few times, he had visited Grand Central Terminal and tried to find his way back into the underworld, but the secret staircase that had led him into it had vanished. He sometimes worried that Euri had moved on to Elysium, the place of everlasting peace, where his mother had gone. But he consoled himself that she would have had to resolve all the problems from her life in order to do that, and it didn't seem likely that could have happened yet.

In Italy, as he sifted through shards and bones, he had finally come to terms with the fact that he might never see Euri or visit the underworld again. It was time for him to put away that chapter of his life and to try to be the ordinary kid he had imagined he would be at Chapman, with close *living* friends and maybe even a girlfriend. It was then that he realized there was only one girl he could imagine himself going out with. And if she read a letter like this—about a trip to the underworld and seeing ghosts—she would think he had lost his mind. He tore up the letter and threw it away.

As Cora chatted about his other letters, Jack felt relieved that he had kept these secrets to himself. But even if she didn't think he was crazy, it was still hard to ask her out. What if she didn't really like him? What if she said no?

Jack opened his mouth, but it was too late. Out of the corner of his eye, he saw Ellen hurrying toward them. "Hey," she said to Cora, squinting through her glasses and gesturing across the Pinetum. "Isn't that Austin?"

Jack stared with annoyance at the tall, spiky-haired figure walking toward them. Even though he was a junior, Austin Chapman, the great-grandson of the school's founder, was also in Jack's Latin class. Whenever Jack saw him, he seemed to have his arms around the skinny, blond girls who took French and never spoke to Jack.

"Yeah," said Cora in an unsurprised voice.

Ellen turned to her. "What's he doing here?"

"I invited him," said Cora, with a mischievous grin. "He wanted to come."

"To hang out with *us*?" Ellen asked.

Cora shrugged. "Why not?"

Jack felt his stomach tighten. It was clear why Austin was coming to hang out with them. Jack wasn't the only one who had noticed Cora and how she somehow seemed more alive than the rest of the girls at Chapman. He dug his fingers into the grass, wishing he had asked Cora out when he had had the opportunity. Gene and

Misha wandered over, exchanging puzzled looks. By the time Austin reached them, everyone had grown quiet.

"Hi," Austin said. He smiled at Cora and gave little half-waves to everyone else.

"You want to sit?" Cora asked.

Austin shrugged. "Sure."

As Austin sat down next to Cora, Jack could see Ellen mouth to Gene, *What is he doing here?*

"So this is Latin Club," Austin remarked, in a tone that implied he was already bored.

"Oh, come on," said Cora with a laugh. "It's fun."

They all stared silently at Austin. Jack knew they didn't seem the least bit fun.

"We're working on next week's translation," said Gene, finally. Everyone else looked at him, surprised that someone new had spoken. "It's the Proserpina myth."

"I haven't even finished this week's," said Austin.

"But you already know the story, right?" Gene asked.

"It's about not eating in the underworld or something like that."

"Exactly," said Cora. "Pluto kidnaps Proserpina and takes her to his kingdom in the underworld. Her mother, the goddess of the harvest, wants her back. Jupiter agrees, but before Pluto can release her she eats six pomegranate seeds."

"Seven, in Ovid," said Jack before he could stop himself.

"Well, most of the time it's six," said Cora. "Anyway, so for half the year she has to stay in the underworld. And that's when it becomes winter, because her mother mourns."

Austin smiled at her. Jack dug his fingers deeper into the grass. He couldn't believe Austin was just going to show up one day—the *very* day he had chosen to ask Cora out—and steal her away. He had to do something to stop him. He turned to Gene. "Hey, what lines were you guys having trouble with?"

"Tartara quid cessant? Cur non matrisque tuumque imperium profers?" said Gene.

Jack translated the lines in his head effortlessly. Venus, the goddess of love, says them to her son, Cupid, to encourage him to shoot an arrow of love at Pluto: *Why is the land of the dead exempt? Why not extend our empire into their realm?* Jack found it interesting that, although there were many versions of the Proserpina myth, only Ovid's blames Venus for Proserpina's abduction. But instead of discussing this with Cora, he pretended to look perplexed. "I haven't gotten that far. Maybe Austin can help?"

Ellen gave him a funny look.

"Or I can," said Cora.

"I can do it," said Austin. "Where's your book?"

"On the table," said Gene.

As Jack watched Austin follow Gene back over to the

picnic table, he fought a smile. His plan had worked out perfectly. Austin was one of the worst Latin students in their class. It would take him a while to figure out the line. Ellen and Misha trailed after Austin, and Cora got up to join them.

"Wait," said Jack, lightly touching her arm. "Do you want to hang out tomorrow night?"

Jack could hear his heartbeat whooshing in his ears. He was certain his face was red again.

"Sure," said Cora.

Jack realized that he must have looked surprised, because she gave him a reassuring smile. "Yeah, that would be fun."

Jack tried to act like her answer wasn't a big deal. "Want to meet at Seventy-ninth and Broadway at six?"

As soon as he said it, Jack wondered if he should have offered to pick her up. But he'd never been to Cora's apartment, and she had never invited him over. The Latin Club had never met there, either.

"Sounds like a plan," said Cora.

To Jack's relief, before he needed to say anything else, Cora's cell phone rang.

"*Hola, Mama,*" she said. Jack could hear a voice rising and falling on the other end. "I know it's getting dark. I know. Okay. I'm heading home," she continued in a disappointed voice. "See you soon."

Shutting off her phone, she stood up. "My mom," she said, apologetically. "I have to go."

As the lights began to switch on in the park, Jack watched Cora say good-bye to Austin. He couldn't hear exactly what they said but, in the middle of it, Austin nodded at him. Jack realized he'd been staring and, after a nod in Austin's direction, he turned away. Even though Cora had agreed to go out with him, Jack felt unsettled. Perhaps it was just the early autumn darkness, so incongruous on such a warm day.

"*Vale*, Jack!" said Cora as she hurried out of the park with Ellen.

"*Vale!*" he replied.

"Hang out? That's some invitation."

An unfamiliar voice startled Jack. He turned to see a small, stout African American woman in a gray flannel dress floating beside him in the blue evening light. She had translucent brown eyes, shiny, dark skin, and was wearing a white bonnet over her graying hair. Remembering what Euri had told him, about how most ghosts would be rattled by someone living noticing them, Jack quickly looked away.

The ghost laughed softly to herself. "That child probably didn't even know she was being courted."

Jack jumped to his feet. "I've got to go, too," he called out to the others. "See you guys later."

"I'll walk out with you," Austin said, getting up from the table.

"I'm late," Jack said lamely. He took off as fast as he could across West Drive, past Spector Playground, and back toward Mariner's Gate. But the ghost floated effortlessly alongside him and, when Jack stopped at Central Park West to wait for the light, the ghost flew around him so she could peer directly into his face. "What an odd-looking child," she commented.

Jack glared straight at her. "Would you shut up?" he shouted.

He regretted the words the moment they had escaped him. The ghost's eyes widened, and with a shriek, she shot up into the darkening sky.

"Sorry," Jack muttered under his breath. But the ghost, by then, was too far away to hear him. He watched her silhouette zoom back into the park, too frightened to even look back.

Jack tried to laugh the encounter off—there had been something funny about the ghost's shocked expression when she realized that Jack could hear her—but it put him in a bad mood. He realized that the ghost was right— he had sounded pathetic. Cora probably hadn't realized he was asking her out on a date. He would have to explain to her tomorrow how he felt. Or at least come off as more exciting than Austin.

As he walked past the Museum of Natural History and the Rose Center Planetarium, another thought occurred to him. The sun set early now, around six thirty, and most of his date would take place after it. That meant that another ghost could easily decide to join along and become a confidence-crushing third wheel. He imagined sitting at the Lincoln Plaza Cinemas, trying to put one arm around Cora as a ghost guffawed at his attempts. If he were lucky, his paranormal abilities wouldn't work so well, and he wouldn't see ghosts tomorrow night. But there was no way to be sure.

Back in their small apartment on 104th Street, Jack was relieved to find a message from his father, a professor at Columbia University. His note said that he had a faculty meeting and would be working late. Jack needed to talk privately to someone who could help him control his abilities enough so that the spirit world wouldn't ruin his night out with Cora. He picked up the phone and dialed a number he hadn't called in a long time.

II | Ghost Repellent

Augustus Lyons was New York's foremost doctor of the paranormal, though Jack was certain that no one would know it from his shabby office. As he sat in the small, empty waiting room on the twenty-third floor, he wondered how Dr. Lyons even managed to pay the rent. Jack seemed to be his only patient—or his only living one, at any rate. Gladys, Dr. Lyons's ancient, blue-haired secretary, was busy with her usual task of sorting through death certificates. Jack had to clear his throat several times before she even noticed him.

"Dr. Lyons is busy right now," she said without even looking up.

"But he told me to come right over."

Gladys peered over the top of her bifocals and frowned. "You're lucky he was able to squeeze you in on such short notice, Jack. Have a seat."

That was fifteen minutes ago and no one had come into the waiting room or left Dr. Lyons's office since. As he waited, Jack opened up *The Unofficial Guide to the New York Underworld*, a thin book that Euri's friend Professor Schmitt had given him during his visit there. Jack always carried the guide around with him in case he ended up in the underworld again. It explained the real rules to the underworld, the ones that the ghosts who guarded and managed the underworld didn't want anyone to know. Jack turned the fragile pages till he reached a chapter entitled "The Truth About Haunting" and began reading:

"For the most part, the official line on haunting is true—that it is a benign afterlife pastime that has no effect on the living. Unless the living use a Ouija board or other occult means, they cannot see or hear the dead and will only have the barest awareness—a vague feeling, unusual dream, or unbidden memory—of their presence."

Jack snorted. The writers of the *Unofficial Guide* had never factored in a living person like him. He continued reading:

"But there are exceptions to this rule. Occasionally, in theaters, historic dwellings, and other spaces prone to paranormal interference, the dead can have a real impact, creating spots of extreme heat or cold, affecting electrical appliances, moving furniture."

Jack nodded, remembering Edna Gammon, a ghost he had met in the underworld who haunted the St. James Theater and had broken a light and tripped a living chorus girl during a performance of *The Producers*.

"In addition, the newly dead can sometimes temporarily disturb their living loved ones, hiding car keys, causing the telephone to ring, and, a particular favorite, messing with alarm clocks. In rare cases, usually after a tragedy has divided the living and the dead, this type of paranormal interference can continue for months or even years (see *Who Moved My Glasses?: Confessions of a Poltergeist* by Molly Mellon Minks)."

"We should have gone out the window," a voice hissed.

Jack looked up. An impatient-looking man in a bowler hat and mustache was floating across the waiting room next to a stately woman in a bell-shaped dress carrying a pink lace umbrella. "If one of the guards were to see us . . ." the man continued in a tense whisper.

"Pish posh," interrupted the stately ghost. "We would just tell them we were going for a stroll."

"Dr. Lyons has a talking board!"

"Is it our fault what the living play with?" the lady ghost said with an uninterested yawn.

"You wouldn't take that view if the guards saw your hand on the indicator—" The ghost in the bowler hat suddenly caught Jack staring at him. Jack quickly turned away. "This place gives me the willies. I could have sworn that boy just saw me."

"Please, Mortimer," said the woman in the bell-shaped dress. She jabbed her umbrella at Jack, who flinched.

"Did you see that?" roared the man.

"Sorry," Jack squeaked, turning to face them.

The lady ghost screamed and fainted into her companion's arms.

Gladys peered curiously at Jack. "Did you say something?"

"Just talking to myself," he said.

Jack turned back to the ghost in the bowler hat. "I'm perfectly harmless. . . ." he whispered. But with a terrified expression, the ghost flew through the wall, carrying the limp woman.

With a sigh, Jack settled back into his seat. How would he ever explain a moment like that to Cora? Just like Gladys, she would think he was crazy.

"Hello, Jack." Dr. Lyons's obese form loomed in the waiting-room doorway. "Why don't you come on in?"

Jack followed Dr. Lyons down the dimly lit hall and into his office. A haze of candle smoke drifted through the air, making it smell like a birthday party had just taken place. The office was just as ramshackle as the last time Jack had been there, lined with rows of crumbling leather-bound books with fading titles and sagging spines. The only nice object was a bookcase made of lifelike tree limbs that contained Dr. Lyons's collection of tokens, Playbills, baseball cards, and other New York memorabilia. On his first visit to Dr. Lyons's office, Jack had found his golden bough, the object that gave him passage to the underworld, in this bookcase. It had been an old subway token that flashed gold. But this time, nothing on the shelves sparkled or glittered. A Ouija board lay on Dr. Lyons's desk, next to one of the still-smoking candles. Dr. Lyons gestured for Jack to sit down on his worn couch. "So," he said, lowering himself into his armchair, "what did they look like?"

"Who?" said Jack, even though he had a feeling he knew who the doctor was talking about.

"The spirits. The ones you saw in the waiting room."

"How did you know I could see them?" Jack asked.

Dr. Lyons chuckled and pulled out his bulky 1947 Polaroid camera. The flash briefly lit up the room and left dancing white lights in Jack's eyes. Dr. Lyons bent over the developing photo. After a moment, he held it up so Jack could see. Jack looked overexposed—his face and body were nearly transparent—but the rest of the photo looked perfectly normal. "You still have your powers," Dr. Lyons remarked.

Jack nodded. "She was tall. She looked like someone from the nineteenth century. Someone wealthy. He was shorter with a mustache and a hat."

Dr. Lyons laughed. "She said she was a maid."

Jack looked confused.

"A lot of spirits lie," he explained. "Or conceal things."

Jack thought about Euri and how she had kept both her real name, Deirdre, and her suicide a secret until he had spent several days with her. He often wondered what else she hadn't told him. But Euri wasn't why he was here.

"The reason I wanted to see you is that I can't control it," he said. "I mean I can't control when I see ghosts. Some nights I do and some I don't."

Dr. Lyons opened up Jack's patient file and took notes. When Jack was finished, Dr. Lyons looked up. "Your powers may be developing as you grow. Or fading. I'm afraid I can't tell which. You're the only patient I have with abilities like this."

Jack frowned.

"But why does it bother you? If the spirits are troubling you, Jack, you just have to learn to ignore them."

Jack felt the color rush to his face. "Tomorrow night," he blurted out, "I have something to do. I just want them to go away. For a little while."

Dr. Lyons's eyes twinkled, and Jack wondered if he guessed he was meeting a girl. "Very well," he said, heaving himself out, of his chair. "Let's see what we can do for you."

Dr. Lyons waddled over to his bookshelves and traced a pudgy finger along the rows of titles. He slid a plain little volume with a cross on the front of it from the shelf. "*Saints, Demons, and Mysteries of the Church,*" he read, and opened it up. "Now, let's see. Ghosts, ghosts, ghosts. Yes . . . 'Those frequently troubled by spirits should pray to St. Dymphna, patron saint of mental disorders.'"

"I'm not crazy," protested Jack.

Dr. Lyons stuffed it back onto the shelf. "You're right. Not helpful."

Next, he produced a smaller book with Chinese characters embossed in gold on the front. He flipped through a few pages and then stopped. "'This is an ancient feng shui remedy,'" he read. "'Keep a mirror with you at all times. If the spirit sees itself in the mirror, it will become frightened and leave.'"

Jack imagined carrying a mirror around with him on his date and flashing it in front of him. "Is there anything less . . . obvious?" he asked.

Dr. Lyons went back to studying his collection of paranormal books. "Ah, here we go," he finally said, pulling a slender, peeling volume from the shelf and holding it up for Jack. *Night Watch* by Lodowyck Pos was written in elaborate script on the front cover. "Lodowyck Pos. This should do it."

"Who's Lodowyck Pos?" Jack asked.

Dr. Lyons flipped through the book. "He lived in the city when it was a Dutch colony and a pretty wild place.

In 1658, he organized a precursor to the police department called the Rattle Watch, a group of citizens who patrolled the streets at night. Occasionally they would have run-ins with ghosts, mostly those of Lenape Indians. Here, I'll read you what he advises."

Dr. Lyons cleared his throat. "'Our watch did have occasion to encounter spirits, both young and old, which gave a great fright to our company. An Indian woman, hearing of our plight, offered a remedy of such good effect that I made certain that my entire company carried a supply in a small pouch. It contained: one bulb of garlic, one bunch of five-finger grass, one stick of cinnamon, one leaf of echinacea. During our watch, no person possessed of this remedy was troubled by a spirit presence.'"

Jack gave Dr. Lyons a skeptical look. "So you really think that works?"

"These old folk remedies can be quite powerful," said Dr. Lyons, closing *Night Watch* and putting it back on the shelf. "And it is subtle. You could hide the pouch in a pocket and your girlfr—I mean no one would notice it."

"I'm just going out with friends," said Jack.

"Of course, of course. Whomever you're with won't notice it."

Jack wasn't quite sure something as simple as a bunch of herbs would keep ghosts away, but it was worth a try. He stood up to leave. "Thanks. I should go."

But as he reached the door, Dr. Lyons called his name. Jack turned around. "Yeah?"

"Even if a ghost does try to bother you, remember, you are the one who's alive—and in control."

"Right," said Jack, though he didn't feel that way. Ignoring ghosts didn't seem possible. Shouting at them seemed to work much better. With a quick nod, he left the office, hoping that tomorrow he wouldn't see any ghosts at all.

III | The Worst Date Ever

The next afternoon, back at his apartment, Jack mashed the five-fingered grass, which he had found in Chinatown and looked disappointingly like oregano, with a cinnamon stick, the echinacea his father took when he felt like he was coming down with a cold, and a bulb of garlic. As he was stuffing the concoction into a sandwich bag, his father wandered into their small galley kitchen.

"What's that?" he asked.

Jack peered down at the bag. "It's, uh, for a chemistry project."

"Smells like garlic," his father said, wrinkling his nose.

Jack stuffed the bag into his backpack.

"So, you're enjoying science these days?" his father asked.

Jack nodded.

"Remind me then sometime to show you the cyclotron over at the university."

"What's that?" Jack asked, eager to change the subject.

His father slid onto a stool. "Ever hear of the Manhattan Project?"

"Doesn't it have something to do with the atom bomb?"

"It was the project to make the first one. A group of physicists started it at Columbia during World War II. The cyclotron was one of the first machines they split atoms in."

Jack felt himself becoming interested despite the urge to get his backpack—and the ghost repellent—away from his father. "And it's still there?"

"Part of it supposedly is, a giant electromagnet in the basement of Pupin Hall. The physicists used the network of tunnels under the university to transport radioactive material in and out of Pupin."

"Really?" said Jack.

His father rubbed his hands together, warming to his subject. "The university keeps Pupin locked, but there was a story some years back that a student sneaked down through the tunnels and brought back some uranium. He didn't like his roommate, so he stored it under the guy's bed."

"That sounds like an urban myth," said Jack.

"The roommate did glow for several weeks."

Jack rolled his eyes.

His father chuckled. "Well, just be careful with that

chemistry project of yours. You don't want the same thing to happen to you."

His father ruffled his hair, and Jack pulled away with a grin. "I'm going out with some friends tonight."

"I'm glad to hear it," said his father. He opened his wallet and gave Jack a couple of twenties. "Spend it wisely."

A little after five o'clock, Jack left his apartment and began to walk down Broadway to meet Cora. It had been another unseasonably warm fall day. Along the avenue, old women wheeling metal shopping carts stopped to squeeze the apples and oranges stacked in colorful pyramids outside the delis. Strollers zigzagged around them, the babies inside obscured by string bags sagging with groceries. Students from Columbia, dressed head to toe in black and carrying low-slung messenger bags, drifted toward the subway, heading downtown for the night. A balding man sat on a bench in the median park and read the *New York Times*, which fluttered ever so slightly as cars whizzed past him.

Jack felt the front pocket of his backpack, reassuring himself that the ghost repellent pouch was inside. He glanced at himself in a store window. Even though he had just showered, the gel he had used for the first time made his hair look greasy. He walked on, checking the time on the pocket watch the poet Dylan Thomas had given him during his visit to the underworld. He tried to slow his pace, not wanting to be too early.

In his head, he practiced some interesting things he might say, but after a while gave up and concentrated instead on the smells that accompanied a warm day in the city. The doughy scent of H&H bagels; the refrigerated vegetable odor of an air-conditioned grocery store; the fume of hot brake pads drifting up from the subway grate; the sweaty, earthy, pungent smell of . . .

Jack pulled the pouch out of his backpack and sniffed it. A strange odor—like a mix between an Italian restaurant and a public toilet—was emanating from it. Jack stuffed it as deep into his backpack as he could. But now he was worried. He walked a half-block and sniffed again. This time the only thing he smelled was something sweet. He turned and found himself standing in front of a dozen plastic buckets filled with flowers: blue spidery orchids, big red roses, pink speckled lilies, and purple irises with spear-shaped leaves.

That's what he would do. He would get Cora some flowers. Girls loved flowers, and their smell would mask the strange odor of the pouch.

A pretty Korean woman appeared from inside the grocery and flashed Jack an encouraging smile.

"How much are the roses?" he asked. Roses seemed

like a safe choice—girls always wanted to get them for Valentine's Day, and they had a nice smell.

"Eighteen dollars a bunch," the woman said. "I can put a little baby's breath in that. Very pretty for your girlfriend or mother."

Jack looked in his wallet. If he wanted to pay for Cora's dinner, and perhaps a movie, he couldn't spend eighteen dollars on flowers.

The woman noticed his hesitation. "How about the lily? I can make a nice bouquet. Very pretty. Fifteen dollars."

"What do you have for ten?" Jack asked.

The woman grinned. "Oh, I see. You're looking for a bargain. Well, you are in luck." She pointed to a bucket of drooping yellow flowers. "They were shipped yesterday from South America. Because of this hot weather, they arrived a little tired." She propped up one of the yellow heads. "But very pretty, see? Usually they would be expensive—they are a spring flower, but I'll sell you one bunch for five dollars."

"Daffodils?" Jack said doubtfully.

"Narcissus," the woman corrected. "Very pretty. And a nice smell, too."

"Really?" Jack said.

"Better than roses."

Five minutes later, Jack approached Seventy-ninth

Street, gripping the bouquet of narcissus in his sweaty hands. Just as the woman had promised, they had a sweet, cloying smell that had actually started giving Jack a headache. But at least he could no longer smell the pouch. And in a few minutes, he would be handing them over to Cora. When he held them at a certain angle, they didn't even look so wilted.

Up ahead, Jack spotted Cora standing near the subway entrance where they had arranged to meet, chewing vigorously on her gum. She spotted him and waved, and Jack waved back. Seeing her, he no longer felt nervous. She looked excited to see him. As soon as he reached her, he handed her the bouquet.

"Wow, flowers," said a voice a few yards away. Jack turned to see Austin leaning against the subway entrance railing. To Jack's dismay, he was very much alive.

"Shut up, Austin!" said Cora. But her eyes widened. "For me?"

Jack felt his face grow hot. He thrust the bouquet into Cora's outstretched hands.

Austin joined them and gave Jack a light punch on the forearm. "Maybe I should leave you two alone."

That would be nice, Jack thought. But instead he turned to Cora. "They were on sale," he muttered help-lessly.

Cora's mouth twisted, and Jack couldn't tell whether

she was embarrassed or trying not to laugh. "Ellen was supposed to come, too, but she had a sore throat," she explained. After an awkward moment, she held up the drooping bouquet. "Thanks for these, Jack. They're really nice."

Jack wondered if he could just go home. His date, which had never really been a date in the first place, was ruined. He didn't even need a ghost to tell him that.

"What's that smell? You wearing cologne, Jack?" asked Austin with a sly wink in Jack's direction.

"It's the flowers," said Cora, sniffing at the bouquet.

Austin wrinkled his nose. "No, something else. It must be from the subway. Let's go."

"Where?" asked Cora.

Austin shrugged. "We could go to my place."

Jack knew that Austin lived in an enormous apartment in the Beresford, one of the fancy buildings on Central Park West.

Cora blew a bubble. "Sound okay, Jack?"

Jack was about to lie and say it sounded fine when he thought of Euri. The Jack that Euri had known wouldn't just give up. He'd find a way to compete with Austin and win Cora over. The first step was to keep her out of Austin's fancy apartment and take her somewhere just as exciting. "Or we could go to Columbia," he said.

"Is there a party over there?" asked Austin, looking intrigued.

"Something better," said Jack. "Have you guys ever heard of the Manhattan Project?"

"Sure," said Austin. "It was the project to build the first atom bomb. My great-grandfather worked on it."

"Really?" asked Cora.

"No joke. He was this physics genius."

Jack tried to ignore Cora's impressed look. "There's still a part of the project, this machine called the cyclotron, hidden in the basement of Columbia," he said. "Not many people know about it. But if you guys want to do a little urban exploring, I can take you there."

"I don't know . . ." Austin started to say.

"They sometimes have secret parties down there," Jack added. "Really crazy ones."

This was a lie, but he knew Cora wouldn't call him on it. She hadn't been to any crazy parties either—not with her mom checking in on her all the time.

"I'm in," said Austin.

"Cora?"

Cora gave him a skeptical look, and, for a second, Jack thought his plan had failed.

"Oh, why not?" she finally said with a snap of her gum. "A little urban exploring. And then we can go to Austin's when we're done."

IV | The Manhattan Project

"This way," said Jack, pointing to a set of maroon doors. They were standing in the basement of Schermerhorn, the four-story brick-and-stone building at Columbia University that Jack's father worked in. The long basement hallway was empty, and the only sound was the buzz of the lights above their heads. Against the wall were faculty mailboxes, including one with his father's name on it.

"This is totally creepy," said Cora with an impish smile.

Jack did a quick check to make sure no one else was in the hallway, then pushed open the doors revealing a second, narrower hall lined with gray industrial-looking lockers. He had noticed it once before when a janitor had left the maroon doors ajar. On the left, just past the lockers, was an open door. Inside it was a room lined with thick white pipes and electrical pumps that breathed heavily in and out. A set of gray cement stairs led down into it. "I'm pretty sure this is an entrance to the tunnel system," Jack said. "If we follow it across campus we should be able to get into the basement of the Pupin building, where the cyclotron is."

"I thought you said you'd been there before," said Austin.

Jack shrugged as he started down the stairs. "I went a different way."

"This'll be fun," said Cora. She held the bouquet of narcissus upside down, but Jack didn't mind. At least she still had them. "Ellen is going to be so sad she didn't come," she added.

At the bottom of the stairs, Jack spotted another door that led into a passageway. Huge steam pipes lined the ceiling, and a few naked bulbs illuminated the red brick walls. It seemed to extend on and on, narrowing into the darkness. "How far does it go?" asked Cora as she peered down it.

"Pretty far," said Jack vaguely. As Cora and Austin walked ahead of him, he pulled the *Unofficial Guide* out of his backpack and opened it up. Inside the back cover he had carefully folded a copy of Egbert Viele's topographical map of New York. Viele had been the city's top engineer, and the map, which he drafted in 1865, was his masterpiece. It showed all the streams and rivers that had ever existed in Manhattan. On his trip to the underworld, Jack had discovered that Viele's map also included secret underground rivers and streams that could be used to get in or out of the underworld. But they were never marked, and certain rules had to be followed—for example, having a golden bough—to use them.

Jack studied the map and found 119th and Amsterdam, where Schermerhorn was. There were no rivers or streams beneath it, but there was one, he noticed, that began a block to the north and west under Pupin.

When he looked up, Austin and Cora had wandered deeper into the tunnel and were staring at something on the wall. Jack hurried over to them and found that they were reading some graffiti neatly written in white paint.

The Road goes ever on and on
Down from the door where it began.

"Hey, isn't that from *The Lord of the Rings*?" said Cora.

Jack nodded. "It's the hobbit walking song."

"My brother loved those books," said Austin.

Cora turned to look at him. "I didn't know you had a brother."

Jack didn't like the surprised tone of Cora's voice, as if she had already secretly learned everything about Austin. But Jack noticed that Austin, too, looked taken aback by Cora's tone. Perhaps he didn't like her as much as Jack feared.

Austin touched the graffiti gently with his fingertips.

"Is he older?" Cora prodded. "Did he go to Chapman, too?"

Austin nodded but didn't offer any details. "Come on," Jack said, waving them forward. "Let's find the cyclotron."

But the passageway, Jack thought, was pretty interesting, too. Some of the pipes also had graffiti on them. In several places, loose electrical wires hung from between them like small black snakes. A few of the pipes gurgled softly overhead, as if they were in the midst of digesting something large inside them. The passageway was neat and clean-swept, though they occasionally saw unlabeled metal barrels, coils of hoselike tubing, and what looked like wooden door frames propped against the walls.

"You guys are so good at Latin," Austin said in his usual laid-back tone. "Why do I have to bust my butt for a B?"

"Nemo Romanus adest qui locutionem tuam corrigant," said Cora.

Not one Roman is around to correct your pronunciation. Jack grinned.

Austin looked confused, but as he slowly translated the line, he started to smile. "Mr. O'Quinn is tougher than any Roman."

"I can help you," Cora offered.

Austin looked at her and smiled. "That would be really great."

"I could help you, too," Jack said. He didn't really want to help Austin, but he didn't like the idea of Cora being alone with him.

Just then, the passageway intersected with another one. Jack hesitated. He knew that Pupin, the building with the cyclotron, was northwest of his father's building, but he had lost his sense of direction underground. Taking a guess, he pointed at the passageway that veered left. "It's this way."

This next passageway had lower ceilings and the pipes were smaller. Threads of yellow insulation hung off them. As they ventured deeper into it, Jack stopped to show Cora how in some places the mortar had crumbled, the bricks had loosened, and underneath it were big rough-hewn stones. "Probably the original foundation," he said.

Austin peered down the passageway. "Are you sure we're going the right way?"

There was an uncertain, even worried, note in Austin's voice, and Jack hoped that Cora had also noticed it. "Of course I'm sure."

Cora pulled her cell phone out of her pocket. "There's no way we can get lost down here," she remarked. "Mine still works. But this passageway looks really old."

"What time is it?" asked Jack.

Cora looked at her phone. "Almost six thirty."

Outside, Jack realized, the sun had set.

Cora suddenly grinned. "I wonder if there are ghosts down here."

"What?" said Jack, glancing around.

"Ghosts! Like whoooooooo . . . Look at the two of you!"

Jack looked at Austin. His eyes were wide, but when he caught Jack looking at him, he smiled sheepishly.

"Whoooo," Cora continued, laughing.

"Elocution lessons," a man's voice intoned from behind him. "An excellent moral treatment for the patients."

Jack swung around. A stooped man with a pinched, pale face was floating toward them through the tunnel. Accompanying him was an older, plump man with glasses. "So, Dr. Earle, you advise it along with exercise and weekly lectures?" he asked.

"And parties and dancing," Dr. Earle continued. "At Bloomingdale we believe in treating our patients as if they were still in the enjoyment of the healthy exercise of their mental faculties. Now, tell me about your own work."

The ghosts seemed largely unaware of Jack's presence—and ignored Cora and Austin as well. But Jack didn't want to take any chances. He dug the pouch of ghost repellent out of his backpack and held it in the air.

The effect was instantaneous. Austin and Cora covered

their noses, and from behind him, Jack heard gagging and coughs.

"What is that smell?" demanded the plump ghost.

Cora pointed to the pouch. "What *is* that?"

"That's it! That's what I smelled before," said Austin, waving his hand in the air.

Jack turned, expecting the ghosts to flee, but they just stood there waving their hands over their noses. "If you weren't dead," the plump ghost said to Dr. Earle, "I might have thought that was you."

The two ghosts erupted into laughter. Jack felt mortified. He looked at Cora and then at the pouch in his hands. "It's just, uh, my allergy medication. It's . . . homeopathic."

"You never told me you had allergies," Cora said. She held up the limp bouquet of narcissus. "Is it the flowers?"

"I can't take it anymore," said the plump man. "Shall we head back to your office?"

Dr. Earle wrinkled his nose. "A fine idea."

The two ghosts floated hastily in the opposite direction.

"No, it's not the flowers," Jack said. "It's . . . to invisible things."

Austin grimaced. "My mother's like that—with dust mites. But she takes some prescription stuff. I know it doesn't smell like that."

"Sorry," mumbled Jack. He shoved the pouch back into his pocket. The ghost repellent had worked . . . sort of. The ghosts had left him alone, but he noticed that Cora and Austin had also backed away from him. The pouch wasn't going to be a practical method of keeping ghosts away unless he wanted to keep the living away, as well. He continued down the passageway, Cora and Austin following at a safe distance. He needed to find the entrance to Pupin soon so they would forget about the smell. He hoped the electromagnet looked as impressive as he imagined. He would have to explain why there was no party tonight, but he knew it wouldn't matter much to Cora, anyway. He visualized the door to Pupin—imagining white letters stenciled on it—and hoped it would appear. But there were no doors along this passageway. Up ahead, Jack noticed that the ground turned dark and shimmery, and as he got closer, he realized it was wet.

"It's flooded," Austin said. "Maybe we should turn back."

But Jack barely heard him. The tunnel wasn't flooded. They had found the underground stream on the Viele map. He saw the bony, old face of a man with a scruffy beard reflected in the water.

"Great," Austin whispered. "Now the janitor's busted us."

The old man, who was dressed in a dark green

uniform that read *Columbia University Janitorial Staff*, stared soundlessly at the three of them. Then he held out one sinewy hand.

Even though he was dressed differently from the last time Jack had seen him, Jack instantly recognized Charon, the gatekeeper to the underworld. According to the *Unofficial Guide*, a living person could only see Charon, and be offered entry into the underworld, if he possessed a golden bough. Jack knew they must have the golden bough with them, but he hadn't seen anything shine or sparkle. He rooted through his backpack. All he could find were the remaining bills from his father, the ghost repellent pouch, and the *Unofficial Guide*. None of them looked like a golden bough.

"What does he want?" Cora whispered behind him.

"I think he wants us to go," Austin said.

"I think you're right," said Cora.

She turned to leave. But Jack couldn't let her. Before he could stop himself, he grabbed Cora's elbow. She started and dropped the bouquet of narcissus, which scattered across the ground. "Let's go a little farther," he said.

"Jack, are you crazy?" Cora whispered. "The janitor is right..." She turned around to look at Charon, but he was no longer standing in front of them. Instead, he had squatted down and picked up three of the yellow narcissus, which he wound in a piece of string and stuck in his front pocket. With a smile full of broken teeth, he stood up, waded through the water, and disappeared down the tunnel.

"That was completely weird," Cora said when they could no longer see him.

They were in—all of them. Jack hesitated at the edge of the stream. All they had to do was walk across the water, and he could show Cora something more amazing than the cyclotron: a place where he had powers that no other living person had.

But then he reminded himself of the underworld guards always searching for living intruders with the help of Cerberus, the three-headed, flesh-eating dog. *Turn around*, Jack told himself. *Take Cora home.* But she wouldn't want to go home, he reminded himself. She'd want to go to Austin's. And if she went to Austin's fancy apartment, there would be no chance of winning her back. Jack looked at her. Her cheeks were slightly flushed, and her dark eyes studied his. He could just take her for a few minutes and bring her back when they were done.

"Come on," he said, holding out his hand to her. "There's something I want to show you."

V | The Best Date Ever

"Do you know that old guy?" Cora asked.

"Sort of," said Jack. "Anyway, he won't bother us any-more. Come on, we're almost there." He took Cora's hand. It was warm and a little bit sweaty. She didn't look surprised, and Jack suddenly wished he'd had the courage to grab her hand before. "Ready?" he said as he led her into the flooded part of the tunnel.

The lukewarm water seeped into their shoes, but Jack was barely aware of it. All he could feel was Cora's hand in his own. He couldn't bear to look at her directly, so he glanced at her reflection in the water. "You're crazy," she said, but Jack detected a hint of admiration in her voice.

"Maybe we should head back now," Austin called from behind them.

Jack turned to see that Austin was still standing in the dry part of the tunnel. "It's not much farther," Jack said.

Austin hesitated, then sloshed his way toward them through the water.

"You know I never get scared," Cora boasted.

"I didn't think you were."

Cora lowered her voice. "I think Austin is, though."

"Just a little," whispered Jack, trying hard not to sound happy.

"I wonder why he's never mentioned his brother before?"

Jack felt briefly annoyed. "I don't know. Maybe they don't get along."

"Maybe," said Cora. She whispered in Jack's ear, "Or maybe something happened to him."

The water grew shallower. Another ten feet and they were back on dry ground. This part of the passageway looked much the same as it had before: low piping, old stone foundation, narrow walls. Jack continued on for a little while, following the tunnel around a bend, just in case any guards were on watch duty by the water's edge. But he also needed time to gather his courage. He hoped that what he was about to do was just like riding a bicycle—easy to remember after a long break—because he knew it would impress Cora more than anything that Austin could ever do.

Finally, when the flooded part of the tunnel was out of sight, he stopped. "I'm going to show you something now, but don't get frightened," he told Cora.

She put one hand on her hip. "I told you I don't

get frightened. Maybe of Mr. O'Quinn a little, but that's about it."

Austin caught up with them. "So where's the cyclotron? Are we there?"

Jack ignored him. "Promise me?" he asked Cora.

"I promise. What are you going to do?"

"And keep holding my hand."

She laughed. "It's pretty clammy."

Jack closed his eyes. He tried to picture himself floating, but the ground felt solid beneath his feet.

"What are you doing?" Austin asked. "That janitor guy—"

Just then, Jack heard Cora gasp. He opened his eyes. She was looking down at her feet, which floated several inches above the ground. Jack was floating too.

Austin's mouth fell open and he took a step backward. "What the—?"

"Jack, how did you do that?" Cora shrieked.

"Magic," said Jack.

Austin shook his head, as if snapping himself out of a trance. "This is crazy," he said.

Jack ignored him, and taking Cora's other hand, began to dance her down the tunnel, spinning her around faster and faster, as they floated above the ground. Austin began to back away.

"Tell the truth," she begged, laughing and kicking her feet in the air.

But Jack didn't want to explain the whole truth to her when they were having so much fun. He worried she would want to leave after she heard it. He spun her around faster, pulling her closer. He felt a sudden urge to kiss her. He closed his eyes.

"Well, if it isn't Fred and Ginger," a familiar voice piped up from behind him.

VI | Bloomingdale

Jack opened his eyes and let go of Cora.

"Ouch!" she shouted as she landed on her backside on the dirty floor.

Leaning against the wall of the passageway, her arms crossed over her chest, was a pale girl in a plaid skirt and blazer. She had a small, tightly pursed mouth and a dirty-blond ponytail that jutted from her head.

At the sight of her, Austin froze.

"Euri!" Jack exclaimed.

He immediately wanted to tell her everything, to erase the weeks and months they had spent apart. But something was different: Euri looked shorter than Jack remembered. It took him a moment to realize that he had just grown taller. He was older than she was now too, fifteen. He wondered if Euri had noticed the change. He expected her to rush up to him, but she stayed where she was, coolly reclining against the wall.

Suddenly, Austin turned on his heels and began to run.

"Austin, wait!" Jack called after him. "She's a friend!"

Austin stopped and looked back at Euri with a pained expression. "I've got to go," he said, his voice shaking.

"Hold on!" Jack said. "Take this!" He reached into his pocket and tossed Austin the ghost repellent pouch. The noxious smell filled the tunnel as both Euri and Cora held their noses.

Austin obediently caught the pouch and stuffed it in his pocket. Then he took off back down the passageway, disappearing around the bend.

"Who was that?" Euri asked.

"Austin Chapman," Jack explained. "A friend of ours from school."

"Chapman?" Euri repeated. "What a wimp!"

"Do you know him?" asked Cora.

"Why would I know him?" Euri snapped. Jack was taken aback by her tone. Either she had been offended by Austin's reaction to her, or was in a horrible mood, or both.

"Maybe we should go after him?" Cora said as she stood up and rubbed her backside.

"He'll be fine," said Euri dismissively. "Who are you?"

"I'm Cora. Who are you?"

Euri ignored the question, arching her eyebrows in Cora's direction. "Lucky for you, you have padding."

Cora's face turned red.

"This is Euri," Jack weakly offered.

Euri turned to him. "Where have you been?"

The excitement Jack had felt when he first saw her was vanishing fast. "Where have *you* been?"

"That doesn't really matter." Euri shot a glance at Cora. "You've clearly been busy."

Jack felt annoyed with her. It wasn't his fault that he was alive, and that he had continued to grow, or that he had a crush on a living girl who could grow and change with him. But he wasn't the only one upset. Cora's arms were also crossed over her chest, and she was giving Euri the once-over. He had never seen her look so angry.

"What's with the uniform?" Cora asked.

Jack cringed. If there was one thing that Euri was sensitive about, it was having died in her school uniform. Euri clenched her fists and Cora jutted her jaw. But before either of them could say anything else, a piercing howl echoed through the tunnel.

Cora gave Jack a worried look. "What was that?"

"The guards are around," said Euri.

"You mean the janitor?" Cora asked. "Does he have a dog?"

Euri turned to Jack and shook her head. "You didn't tell her, did you?"

Cora looked from Euri to Jack. "What?"

Euri burst into laughter. She laughed so hard, she

clutched her stomach, then curled into a ball and began to float.

Cora grabbed Jack's hand. "What's going on? Why can she fly, too?"

Jack wasn't sure how to answer.

"You're both playing some trick on me. Thanks a lot, Jack. I'm going to go find Austin," Cora said. She turned around and headed back toward the stream.

"Wait!" Jack called after her, but she didn't turn around. He scowled at Euri.

"Okay, okay," she said, pretending to wipe tears from her eyes. "We'll get her."

Jack ran after Cora and Euri flew alongside him. "Would you stop flying?" Jack whispered to Euri just before they reached her.

To Jack's relief, Euri floated back to the ground. They flanked Cora. "What do you want?" she asked.

"You can't leave just yet," Euri said.

"Why not?"

"Because there's a three-headed dog waiting to eat you, if you try to go back now."

"Subtle," Jack mumbled.

But Cora just grinned. "Ha-ha. You must be taking Latin, too. *Cerberus canus Inferorum est.*" She looked at Jack. "You're both in on the joke, right? You really got Austin, but not me. . . ."

"He got out in time," Euri remarked. "You two aren't so lucky."

As if to punctuate her point, a series of barks sounded in the darkness ahead. "They're getting closer," said Euri. "You can follow me or . . . hey, if you want to get eaten . . ." She turned away from them and began to float deeper into the tunnel.

As soon as Euri was out of earshot, Cora turned to him. "Who is that girl?"

Jack peered nervously into the darkness ahead. "I can explain . . ."

Farther down the tunnel, a pair of unblinking red eyes locked on to Jack's. Slightly above the eyes, another pair blinked on, and then a third.

". . . later," Jack squeaked.

Cora followed his gaze over her head. "What are you looking—?"

She gasped and shrank back as Cerberus's three heads began to bark and gnash their teeth simultaneously and pull at a leash.

"Get them!" a low, angry voice shouted.

Jack grabbed Cora's hand, took a few running steps, and flew into the air. They shot through the passageway, the stone walls blurring into gray, Jack's heart furiously pumping in his chest as he gripped Cora's hand. He was flying so fast that they nearly hurtled into Euri, who was floating calmly ahead of them, down a passage-way cluttered with moldering mattresses and rusty gurneys.

"I guess you changed your mind," she said as they screeched to a halt behind her.

"Cerberus," Jack panted. "Go! He's coming."

Euri turned and peered back down the passageway. "I don't see anything."

Jack pointed behind them, but Euri was right—there was no one there, and he could no longer hear barking. The beast must have run in a different direction.

Cora looked frantically from Jack to Euri. "Cerberus," she panted. "We're in hell?"

"I prefer to call it the afterlife," said Euri. "It's got a better ring to it."

"Am I dead?" Cora cried, turning to Jack.

"Here we go again," Euri muttered under her breath.

"When we crossed over that stream, we entered the underworld," Jack explained. "But you're not dead and neither am I. I promise. And we can go back. But if Cerberus catches us . . ." He looked over his shoulder and then imploringly at Euri.

"Okay," she said with an exaggerated sigh. "Euri to the rescue."

"Thank you," said Jack. He noticed that Cora didn't look very relieved by this offer of help. She was staring at

Euri, her eyes widening as she took in their savior's pale skin and the cobwebs on her uniform. But just when Euri had agreed to help them, he didn't want to put her in a worse mood by explaining to Cora that, yes, Euri was indeed dead. "Where are we?" he asked before Cora could say anything.

"In Bloomingdale," said Euri. She turned to Cora. "And don't get your hopes up for a better outfit. It's not the department store."

Cora seemed too rattled to register the insult. She pointed to one of the gurneys. "It's a hospital?"

Euri snorted. "It's an insane asylum. And I've been stuck here for months."

"How are we in an insane asylum?" Cora asked. "I thought we were at Columbia."

"Columbia bought up the asylum and built over it in the 1890s," Euri said in an impatient voice. "But you're in the underworld, remember? And here Dr. Earle still runs Bloomingdale for the dead."

On the word "dead," Cora turned to Jack. "Are you sure there's a way out of here?"

"Of course," said Jack. "We just need to wait a little while till the guards and Cerberus go away. Then we'll go back across the stream like Austin did."

"Isn't there another way out?"

"We have to go back the same way we came in," Jack

explained. "But we'll be able to do that in just a little while. Right, Euri?"

Cora turned to Euri for affirmation, and Jack silently prayed that she wouldn't say anything alarming.

"Sure," Euri said. "You can hang out with me in one of the classes." As she led them into a wider part of the passageway, she added cryptically, "You could definitely use some lessons."

VII | Limbo

A moment later, Euri put a finger over her lips. Jack and Cora nodded to show they understood. The faint beat of an orchestra drifted through the tunnel, then the screech of a needle being dragged over a record, followed by another burst of music. "Just act like everyone else," Euri whispered, "and try not to look anyone in the eye for too long. It's your eyes that give away that you're alive." Pointing at Cora, she added, "You in particular. And if you need to fly or float or anything, you need to hold someone's hand." She vanished through a closed door that Jack hadn't noticed before.

"How did she do that?" Cora whispered.

"She's a ghost," Jack said, now that Euri was out of earshot. "We're going to have to go through it, too, otherwise someone might think we're still alive."

Cora pressed her fingers against the door. "But it's solid. How can we?"

"I'm going to pull you through."

"But you're not a ghost."

"No, but in the underworld I can do ghostlike things—flying and going through walls and—"

Cora jumped as Euri's head popped back through the door. "Are you two going to stand out there all night?"

"Sorry," said Jack. He turned to Cora. "As long as I hold your hand, you can do these things, too." Then, before she could ask him anything else, he flew at the door, pulling her along.

With a gasp, Cora closed her eyes. She and Jack sank into the door, which felt as soft as a mattress before it gave way and dumped them out into a surprisingly cavernous room. Cora opened her eyes and gazed at her arms and legs to make sure they were still there. Jack remembered the feeling himself the first time he went through a solid wall. "You okay?"

Cora nodded, and Jack, satisfied that she still seemed to be in one piece, looked around. Standing in pairs in front of them were about twenty ghosts of all ages and from all eras. A bearded man in a waistcoat and top hat stood across from a woman in a miniskirt and chunky platform heels. A woman in a high-collared, floor-length gingham dress stared awkwardly at a man in a fedora and broad-shouldered gray suit. A girl in jeans and a T-shirt loosely held the hand of a man with a Mohawk who wore nothing more than a loincloth made of animal skin.

In the corner, a tall ghost in a flouncy white shirt, knickers, and high-heeled shoes bent over a record player with an enormous hornlike speaker. "Technology," he muttered to himself. "You can never keep up with it."

"Are they all . . . *exanimus*?" Cora whispered.

Dead. Jack nodded at the Latin word.

Cora shuddered. "Why can I see them, then?"

"Because you're in the underworld."

"And they can see me?"

Jack nodded. "But remember, don't stare too long, because they might notice that you're not really dead."

Just then a diminutive African American man, barely up to Jack's shoulder, strode through the door. He wore a pair of plaid pants, white shoes, and a white-collared shirt.

Euri floated up to them. "The weekly guest instructor," she said flatly.

The tall ghost stopped fiddling with the record player and clapped his hands with excitement. "Ladies and gentlemen!" he announced. "We have a very special guest for you today, the inventor of the greatest dance in all of eternity—George 'Shorty' Snowden!"

A weak scattering of applause echoed through the room as the small ghost held out his arms, beaming. "We're going to do the Lindy Hop," he explained, "the dance I invented myself at the Savoy Ballroom. So get yourself a partner if you don't have one already."

Jack turned to Euri. "This is a dance class?"

Euri shrugged. "It's part of the therapy. Dr. Earle likes us to stay active."

The tall ghost floated up to Jack. "Looks like you have one partner too many," he remarked. Turning to Cora, he held out his hand. "You remind me of a girl I knew when I was alive. Shall we?"

Cora gave Jack a worried look.

"Sorry," Jack explained to the ghost. "But I'm sure Euri would love to . . ."

Euri glared at Jack as the tall ghost bowed and offered her his hand.

"All right," said Shorty, lowering the arm of the record player. "And a one, two . . ."

On three, the orchestra struck up, and pairs of ghosts shot into the air, kicking, hopping, shaking, sliding, and spinning each other in a mad mixture of waltzes, lambadas, jigs, break-dances, fox-trots, and disco. As Jack floated into the air with Cora, he concentrated less on dancing and more on avoiding a kick in the face.

"We have some work ahead of us," Shorty observed.

"That's an understatement," Euri muttered as she whirled by on the arms of the tall ghost, who seemed to be doing some sort of minuet.

"So this is what happens after death?" Cora whispered. "Bad dancing?"

Jack was relieved that she seemed a little more relaxed. "I hear everyone's a lot better by the time they reach Elysium."

For a brief moment, Cora smiled. Then her expression grew serious. "You said you could do all these ghostlike things in the underworld. That means you've been here before."

Jack took a deep breath. Then he whispered the story of how he had been hit by a car and started seeing ghosts. He explained how he had met Euri at Grand Central Terminal and how she had led him to the underworld. He told Cora about the search for his mother and how he had helped her move on to Elysium, the place of eternal peace, which was likely in the Hamptons. He told Cora about how, even when he wasn't in the underworld, he could still see ghosts at night.

"How come? What's wrong with you?" she asked.

"I don't know," he said. "I would have told you all of this sooner, but I figured you'd think I was crazy."

Cora's eyes surveyed the ghosts dancing around the room. "I probably would have. But I still kind of think you're crazy now."

Jack's face felt hot, and he looked over her shoulder so she wouldn't see. He was relieved he hadn't sent her his letter. It was painful enough telling her the truth now. He watched as Shorty floated from couple to couple, correcting their steps—often a difficult matter as one ghost was doing a Viennese waltz, and the other the Macarena. Behind him, he noticed a few chairs set against the walls. Just above one of them floated a grizzled peg-legged ghost reading a newspaper called THE UNDERWORLD TIMES. Jack could just make out a large banner on the front of it that read MANN DOWN EXCLUSIVE!!! and beneath it a headline: LIVING AVENGER STRIKES AGAIN!!! CENTRAL PARK VICTIM SAYS, "MOST TERRIFYING MOMENT OF MY DEATH."

Jack nearly crashed into the man with the Mohawk. He was too far away to read the rest of the story, but he could make out a panel of photos accompanying it. There was one of Bigfoot, another of the Loch Ness monster, and the third was a primitive sketch of a pair of glowing eyes set in an alien-shaped face. A caption below read LIVING AVENGER: MYTH OR MENACE? Jack tried to dance closer to the newspaper, but before he could make out anything more, Shorty flew up to them.

"You're too stiff," he observed.

"Well, we *are* dead," Jack said with a forced laugh.

Shorty clapped his hands, and someone dragged the arm of the record player across the record so the music screeched to a halt. "If you fine people are going to learn to Lindy Hop," Shorty announced, "then you're going to have to loosen up. Time to limbo!"

"Hooray!" shouted the tall ghost, releasing Euri's hand and pumping his long arms. Euri took the chance to flee back to Jack and Cora. "Welcome to limbo," she said to Cora with a roll of the eyes. Then she turned to Jack and hissed in his ear, "Thanks for that last dance."

Jack could tell she was hurt. He hadn't imagined their reunion going this way at all. But he needed to protect Cora and make sure she got out of the underworld quickly and in one piece. "Cora couldn't dance with one of the others," he explained gently. "They might figure out who she is."

Euri picked at her skirt. "So?"

"Let's get into a single file line," Shorty instructed. He flew over to the record player and slipped a new album out of its jacket. The steel drums and rattles of calypso flooded the room. The man with the Mohawk and the woman in the floor-length dress produced a pole and floated ten feet into the air with it. Jack and Cora exchanged alarmed glances. "Go to the back of the line," Jack whispered. He let go of Cora's hand and watched her walk to the back.

"Let's start with you, miss," Shorty said, pointing to Euri.

As Euri levitated, Jack was surprised she was being such a good sport. But then, instead of floating under the pole, she danced through it. "That's cheating," murmured the woman in the miniskirt, and Euri stuck her tongue out at her.

"Let's have good clean fun here," the tall ghost said with a disappointed look at Euri. "You, young man, are next."

"Me?" said Jack.

"Time to limbo," said Shorty.

Jack closed his eyes and willed himself a few feet up into the air. Then he floated stiffly under the pole.

"Great!" said Shorty, although Jack knew he was probably the least animated dancer in the history of the limbo. "Let's mix up this line, get some of the shy folks up here." He pointed to Cora. "How about you?"

Cora stood firmly on the ground, looking anxiously up at the pole.

"Go ahead, miss," Shorty said.

The crowd of ghosts stared quietly at Cora as she turned frantically to Jack. He bit his lip and glanced helplessly at Euri. Cora closed her eyes and began to flap her arms. "What on earth is she doing?" murmured the woman in the floor-length dress.

Just then, Cerberus, dragging a thick-necked guard behind him, barreled through the door. Over the cheerful beat of calypso, ghosts flew helter-skelter through the room, screaming, as Cerberus dashed this way and that, sniffing and growling. The tall ghost shouted to the guard over the din, "Get that beast away! He's not part of the moral treatment! He's upsetting the patients!"

Jack ran up to Cora and grabbed her hand. But as he pulled it, he realized that someone else was pulling her in the opposite direction. It was Euri. "Quick, through the wall," she whispered. Cora winced as they careened toward the brick and into the next room where a small group of ghosts was listening to what appeared—from the title written on a chalkboard—to be a lecture on "Physical, Intellectual, and Moral Beauty."

"As Aristotle argued . . ." a bug-eyed ghost at a lectern was saying.

"Cerberus and the guards are rampaging through Bloomingdale!" Euri shouted.

The room erupted into shrieks as the ghosts shot into the air and several flew out the door. "Calm down!" begged the bug-eyed ghost. But a burst of barking through the wall just increased the pandemonium. Screams began to echo from other parts of the asylum as news spread. "This is perfect!" Euri said, picking up speed as she flew them toward another solid wall. Cora clenched Jack's hand even tighter.

"Are you crazy?" Jack said.

Euri looked as if she was seriously considering the question. "Well, I am in an insane asylum."

For a moment, Jack wondered if Euri really had gone mad. But even if he could wrench Cora from her grip, he had no idea where he would go or how they would escape Cerberus. He wasn't even sure he could find the way back to the stream without Euri's help. It seemed as if they were flying away from Bloomingdale.

"Don't worry," said Euri, looking at the panicked expression on his face. "I'm not really crazy. It's just that you've given us the perfect opportunity to escape." They tumbled through another wall.

"Back to the stream?" asked Cora eagerly.

Euri turned to her. "And get eaten?"

"No, but . . ."

"The guards and Cerberus are going to be all over Bloomingdale for the next few hours. The safest place for you to be till they leave is aboveground."

Cora turned to Jack, a bewildered look on her face. "But wait, if we go aboveground, won't we already be back? Then we'll be safe?"

Jack shook his head. "The dead stay underground during the day, but they're allowed to go up into the city at night. In order to get back to the living world, we can't just join them aboveground, we have to go back the same way we came." He squeezed her hand. "But it's okay. We'll just go up for a couple of hours, till everything settles down, and then we'll go back to the stream. It'll be fine."

Cora looked skeptical. "How are we supposed to get aboveground? I'm not seeing any stairs."

Before Jack could answer, Euri led them around a

corner of the tunnel and flew into a small, dimly lit circular room with earthen walls. On a stool in the middle of it sat an elderly ghost with combed-back white hair and dark eyebrows, reading a book titled *The Moral Obligation to Be Intelligent.* Without even looking up, he pressed a clicker three times. "'What marks the artist is his power to shape the material of pain we all have,'" he murmured to himself.

"Whatever that means," said Euri. She waved goodbye and was instantly sucked into a pipe overhead.

Cora looked at Jack in astonishment. "Just keep holding my hand," Jack shouted as they rose in the air, their bodies flattening as they whirled up through the green copper pipe.

VIII | The Dancing Bear

Jack could hear Cora's screams, but they sounded far off and dreamlike. His fingers, which felt as long and unwieldy as tentacles, twisted around hers. Then suddenly, with a pop, a pungent animal smell filled the air, and Jack was sitting next to Cora in the dark on the lip of a small basin tucked into an alcove. A pair of paws loomed above them, and Jack flinched before he realized it was just a statue of a dancing bear standing on its hind legs.

Euri grinned. "That's why no one likes to take this fountain. The bear reminds them of Cerberus."

Jack smiled as if to show he hadn't really been scared.

"What just happened?" asked Cora.

"We fountain-traveled," said Jack. "The dead use the city's fountains to travel aboveground for the night."

He stood up and looked around. Strange sounds filled the air—braying laughter, spine-tingling roars, high-pitched nonsensical chatter. In front of them was a series of brick arches topped with a clock; on a balcony beneath it, Jack could see the silhouettes of animals: a kangaroo playing horns, a penguin playing a drum, a goat playing panpipes, a hippopotamus playing a violin. It was the Delacorte Clock.

"We're in Central Park," Cora said with a puzzled look.

Jack nodded. "In the zoo." He had walked through it many times on the way home from Chapman but had never seen it at night.

A gate creaked open and a living zookeeper, his head bobbing to the music on his headphones, exited the seal enclosure with a large pail.

"He's going to see us!" Cora said, looking around for a place to hide.

"No, it's okay," said Jack. "He can't. Remember, we're still technically a part of the underworld, so no one living can see us."

Cora watched as the zookeeper walked right past them. Even though he stepped through Jack's foot, his eyes never once shifted in their direction. As soon as he passed, Cora pulled out her cell phone. "I want to call my mom."

"She won't be able to hear you," said Euri.

But Cora was frantically pushing the power button on her phone. "It's dead!"

"Phones don't work in the underworld," Jack explained gently. "But we'll be back before she even knows you're gone."

"She needs to be able to reach me," said Cora.

"Why?" asked Euri.

"Because she does!"

Something bayed from the corner of the zoo. A moment of silence followed before the rest of the animals began to shriek and roar in a deafening cacophony.

Jack turned to Euri. "What was that?"

"New exhibit. Three-headed dog. Let's go."

Euri darted into the air, and Jack grabbed Cora's hand and followed. He could hear Cora suck in her breath as they flew over the Delacorte Clock, their feet grazing the animal band.

"Where should we go?" he asked Euri.

"Probably into the city for a little while," she said, steering them swiftly away from the zoo.

Cora looked uncertainly back over her shoulder. "And then we can go back to that stream, right?"

Euri nodded. "But we should travel back through another fountain." She began to fly west, across the park, sailing higher and higher.

As they rose after her, Cora looked down. "What if I fall?" she asked in a shaky voice.

"You won't," said Jack. "Just hold my hand and enjoy the view."

Beneath them, dark thickets of trees, their leaves still clinging to the branches, gave way to patches of yellow light that illuminated stone bridges and meandering roads, empty playgrounds and shadowy statues. A twinkling line of apartment buildings and luxury hotels encircled the park and beyond them, higher in the sky, helicopters with blue lights darted like dragonflies. Cora's hand was clammy and Jack could feel it pulsing in his own. Below, he caught sight of Bethesda Fountain and flew down to show Cora the ghosts streaming out from beneath the feet of the winged statue of the Angel of the Waters. Hundreds at a time burst into the air in translucent geysers.

Cora's face softened as she tilted her head back to watch. "Every night they do this?"

"Every night," said Jack.

A few child ghosts waved at them and they waved back.

"Good times," remarked Euri with a sour expression. "But there's a guard floating toward the fountain."

She shot into the sky as Jack pulled Cora up after her.

"Wait!" Cora cried, looking down at the terrace.

"What?" Jack asked.

"I think I just saw Austin flying with another ghost!"

Jack looked back just in time to catch the receding silhouettes of a tall figure with spiky hair and a heavy-set ghost. His stomach flip-flopped. "That couldn't be him."

"It looked exactly like him!"

Jack felt annoyed that Cora cared. "But he made it

back," he reminded her. "He's probably at his apartment by now."

"Are you sure?"

"He's fine," Jack insisted. But he wished he felt more certain.

Euri joined them. "What's wrong?"

"Cora thinks she saw Austin fly out of the fountain," Jack explained.

Euri dismissed this with a wave of her hand. "He went back. Trust me. You think he wanted to hang around in the underworld?"

Cora gave her an exasperated look. "You don't even know him."

"Do *you* want to hang around in the underworld?"

"No," Cora admitted.

"Well, just forget about it, then," said Euri. "There are a lot of spirits here. Some of them are bound to look like people you know."

Jack tried to feel reassured. Euri wouldn't let some living kid wander around the underworld. She liked the living. She would have tried to protect him. Cora must have just seen someone who looked like Austin—maybe even a distant ancestor. He touched Cora's shoulder with his free hand. "Don't worry. Austin's fine. And you will be, too. I'll make sure of it."

He turned and saw Euri was staring at them with a

frown. Wayward strands of hair angrily poked up out of her head and her hands were bunched into fists. He realized that he had once said nearly the same thing to Euri—and then failed her. He dropped his hand from Cora's shoulder.

"I have an errand to do," Euri said brusquely before flying ahead of them and out of the park.

IX | The Museum of Unnatural History

"An errand?" Cora said to Jack as they darted after Euri. "*Now*?" She peered down over the snarl of yellow cabs and buses on Central Park West. "You'd better not let me fall."

"I won't." He shook his head, puzzled. "I thought she'd go to the East Side. That's where her parents' apartment is. She used to haunt it."

"Well, she's going to the Museum of Natural History," said Cora. She pointed at Euri, who was hovering above a bronze statue of Teddy Roosevelt atop a horse. Behind her was a building with four enormous Roman-style columns, topped with more statues of scientists and explorers. Giant banners advertising the latest exhibits hung above three padlocked doors. A stream of ghosts disappeared through them.

Jack floated up the stairs with Cora, following Euri through the doors. He felt Cora's grip tighten. "It's okay," he said as he pulled her through. "Look, we're inside."

They were standing in an echoing exhibit hall with a soaring vaulted ceiling. In the center of the hall were towering dinosaur skeletons. Ghosts in white lab coats, tweed jackets, and khakis and pith helmets scurried around them, greeting one another, drawing calculations in the air and waving copies of what appeared to be scientific journals. One group in baggy pants, white shirts, and brown fedoras floated alongside a barosaurus skeleton, taking measurements.

Jack expected Euri to continue on to another hall, but instead she sailed up and disappeared through a tiny door near the top of the ceiling that Jack had never noticed before. Jack pulled Cora into the air and they darted through the closed door after her. They followed her down a stairway and into a room with about twenty cabinets on rails. "Where are we?" asked Cora.

"It looks like some sort of storage room," said Jack. He pulled open one of the cabinet doors. It contained several drawers of carefully catalogued dead beetles. "I think we're in the entomology section."

But Euri didn't stop there. She continued on through another door, past some elevators, and into a windowless hallway, lined with offices. On the floor of the hallway were glass tanks filled with tarantulas and what looked like several different kinds of cockroaches including a large, wingless, brown one. The label on its tank read

"Madagascar Hissing Cockroach." Euri dipped her hand into it.

"What are you doing?" Jack asked.

Euri turned to face them. Her arms were crossed over her chest and her hair looked slightly charged. "Can I have a word with you, Jack?" she said, pointing grimly toward one of the offices.

"Um, sure."

"I'll wait here," Cora offered.

Euri didn't thank her.

Jack followed Euri into an office with a couple of windows. It was filled with colonies of bedbugs in small jars. Jack stood across from Euri. They were finally alone together but it felt all wrong. "What is it?"

Euri suddenly gave him an uncertain look. "Nothing."

"Then why are you . . . ?"

"You didn't call," Euri interrupted with a forced smile. "You didn't write."

"Is this about Cora?"

"Cora?" said Euri as if she'd never heard the name before.

Jack felt the blood rush to his face. "I didn't hear from you for months. I could see other ghosts, but the only one I wanted to see was you. I tried to contact you through the Ouija board. I went to Central Park practically every day looking for you. I even tried to find a way back . . ."

For a moment, Euri's arms uncrossed themselves and the muscles in her face relaxed. But then she scowled and said, "Until you gave up and started hanging around with her!" She jabbed her finger in the direction of the door.

Jack began to feel exasperated. He took a deep breath. "Euri, I'm alive. You have to understand—"

"You're not really alive," Euri interrupted, her voice growing louder. "You can fly by yourself. You can see ghosts. You're a freak! But have it your way." Her pale eyes filled with tears. "Because I'm going!"

"Euri," Jack protested. But it was too late. With an angry swing of her ponytail, she flew out through one of the windows.

Jack floated back through the office door to Cora.

"What happened to Euri?" she asked.

"She left," he said, absently. For a moment, he felt guilty. Euri had been loyal to him, waiting for him to come back, and he had abandoned her for a living girl. But then he thought about what Euri had said—how she had called him a freak. Was that really what she thought of him?

"We'd better follow her," said Cora.

Jack cast an annoyed glance back over his shoulder. "Why?"

A worried furrow appeared in Cora's brow. "Do you know how to get back to that stream?"

X | The Haunted Tenement

As they flew over Central Park after Euri, Jack silently defended himself. *I'm not a freak.* But he didn't feel reassured. The starless sky glowed a faint, eerie pink from the city lights and, as he skirted the tops of trees, racing to keep Euri in sight, flocks of starlings burst from the branches, their wings beating in a collective panic.

"It's me," Cora said. "Euri thinks we're—"

"No," Jack interrupted. "It's not that." Cora was right—of course Euri was jealous. But he couldn't bear to hear Cora dismiss the idea of them being together before he had the chance to tell her he liked her. "She's just being . . ." He hesitated. "Euri."

"How did she die?"

"She killed herself."

He thought Cora would be surprised, but instead she just sighed. "I could never do that to my mom."

"Your mom?"

For a moment, Cora looked flustered. "I mean I

wouldn't do it because I like being alive. But my mom, she's . . . It's just the two of us. My dad left us when I was little."

Jack nodded, hoping Cora would say more. He realized that he had never met her mom—he had only heard Cora talk to her on the phone.

A pained look crossed Cora's face. "If anything ever happened to her, I'd die. I'd keep on living, because that's what she'd want me to do, but inside I'd be dead."

Jack thought about his own mom. "For a little while you'd feel that way. But not forever."

"My mom was the one who found out about Chapman," Cora interrupted, as if she hadn't heard him. "She told me I was smart, that I could go to school anywhere. She even called Mr. O'Quinn and told him that they should recruit me. She would do anything for me. She's the only person in the world I can say that about."

Jack looked at the string of streetlights below that illuminated Literary Walk—a long tree-lined promenade south of Bethesda fountain—and made it look like a tiny landing strip. He wished they could touch down there and he could tell Cora that he would do anything for her, too.

"Why did Euri kill herself?" she suddenly asked.

Jack thought for a minute. "She didn't get along with her parents."

"A lot of people don't," said Cora sympathetically.

"But that doesn't sound like enough of a reason to kill yourself."

Jack had to admit that Cora was right. He had always thought there was more to Euri's story. "I guess she's a bit of a mystery."

"Is her name really Euri? Like Eurydice?"

"She took the name after she died," Jack explained. "When she was alive, her name was Deirdre."

Cora pointed to Euri's silhouette as it veered onto Fifth Avenue. "Do you think we're going to her parents' apartment now?"

Jack shook his head, perplexed. "I think we've already passed it."

They continued to follow Euri as she flew due east, over the Chapman School and Park Avenue and toward tall apartment buildings on the easternmost edge of the city. As soon as they hurtled over these buildings—Cora clutching his hand tight—they could see the snaking line of red brake lights on the FDR Drive, and beyond it, the dark expanse of the East River. Jack knew that New York ghosts couldn't leave the island of Manhattan, but he almost wondered whether Euri was trying to.

Then, just as she neared the river, she veered sharply south, racing over the cars stuck on the crowded highway below and into a different type of traffic—hundreds of ghosts merging and shifting on an aerial freeway.

"Hold on," said Jack as they joined the throng, making sure to stay a dozen or more ghosts behind Euri so she wouldn't notice them. Many of the ghosts were aggressive fliers, cutting in front of Jack and Cora, and nearly causing them to crash.

"On your left, Jack!" Cora shrieked as a ghost in an African tunic nearly rammed into them.

"Watch out!" she shouted as a naked baby in an enormous lace bonnet swerved in front of them.

"I saw the baby," Jack muttered. Cora, he realized, was a backseat flier, and she was making him tense.

But the ghostly traffic moved quickly and they sped through Turtle Bay and past the United Nations. At Houston Street, Euri hung a right and moved westward into the city, flying low past clumps of living teenagers from the projects and hipsters in T-shirts, past the Jewish delis and high-end clothing boutiques and cramped-looking bars. Euri turned onto Ludlow Street and sailed through the window of a four-story brick tenement. Jack put his finger to his lips as he and Cora landed on the fire escape and peeked into the apartment.

The apartment was one of the smallest Jack had ever seen—a single room with a stove and sink at one end and a bed at the other. The phone was unplugged and clothes were scattered across the floor. An unshaven man sat slumped on the bed, a notebook beside him, plucking at a guitar. He was very pale and had dark circles under his eyes, as if he hadn't slept in a long time. "Enjoy this double destruction. . . ." he sang in a whiny tenor.

But before he could finish the line, Euri pulled on one of his guitar strings until it snapped. "Oh, man," he said as the string sprang into the air. "Not again."

With a sigh, he stood up and walked to a guitar case propped against the wall. As he knelt down and pulled a coil of wire from inside it, Euri kicked the case. It fell over and hit him on the head. The man rubbed his head and laughed in an eerie way.

"I can't believe it," Jack said turning to Cora. "Euri's a poltergeist."

"A what?" whispered Cora.

"A poltergeist," Jack repeated. "Normally the dead can't affect the living when they haunt. But if something tragic separated them, the dead can do things to a living person like . . . well, like that." He pointed back inside the apartment. Euri had flown over to the sink and turned on the faucet. The man didn't get up, just dully watched the water blasting into the sink.

"What's wrong with him?" Jack whispered.

"I don't know," said Cora. "He must be someone Euri knew when she was alive."

"He must be. Otherwise she wouldn't be able to haunt him like this."

Cora peered at the man. "How old do you think he is?"

Jack shrugged. "Thirty, maybe?"

"No, he's younger. Maybe twenty-two or twenty-three," said Cora. "And Euri doesn't age, right? When did she die?"

Jack understood. "You're right. They must be around the same age."

It was hard to believe that now, though, since the man's face was lean and defined with the beginnings of a scruffy beard. Euri, in her school uniform and messy ponytail, looked half his age, but Jack knew if she were still alive she, too, would be in her early twenties. As she zoomed over to the light switch and turned it on and off, Jack wondered why the man didn't run out screaming into the night. Instead he sat quietly with his guitar in the flickering light. Euri looked annoyed by his lack of reaction. She reached into the pocket of her jacket and threw something on the floor. It began to hiss loudly like a tiny steam pipe and then quickly scampered into a pile of dirty clothes.

"Was that a cockroach?" Cora asked recoiling from the window.

"A Madagascar Hissing Cockroach," Jack corrected.

Cora screwed up her face. "That's nasty!"

Jack tried to look disgusted, too, but he couldn't

suppress a smile. "I guess we know why Euri went to the museum." He pointed to another hardy-looking roach clinging to the side of the sink and hissing furiously. "Something tells me this isn't the first time she's donated a specimen."

The living man either ignored the new cockroach or didn't see it. He continued to sit stooped and listless over his guitar.

"I hate you!" Euri screamed.

"This isn't right," Cora whispered. "We've got to stop her."

"I . . . HATE . . . YOU!" Euri shrieked, forcing Jack to cover his ears. He peered at a group of living hipsters hanging out on a stoop below. Not a single one looked up.

"I . . . HATE . . ."

Cora let go of Jack's hand and, before he could stop her, she opened the window and scrambled through it. Grabbing Euri by the shoulders, she spoke quietly but firmly. "Stop it!"

Jack flinched, expecting a fight. But, to his surprise, Euri's angry red-faced expression changed into something resembling shame. She looked down at the floor. The man on the bed stood up, turned off the gushing faucet and, with a troubled sigh, closed the window that Cora had left open. For a moment, no one spoke.

Suddenly, a small boy flew through the closed window with a canvas bag on his back, waving a newspaper in his hand. "New Underworld Security Alert!" he shouted. "Mann Down exclusive! Read all about it in a special edition of *The Underworld Times*!!"

The boy tossed a paper to each of them and then looked around at the trashed apartment. "You haven't been haunting, have you?"

"No," said Jack and Euri simultaneously.

The newsboy winked at them and flew back through the window.

"Jack," said Cora, clutching his arm and pointing to the column.

LIVING AVENGER ON THE LOOSE? A MANN DOWN EXCLUSIVE!

Mann Down has just learned that the underworld security team has issued a new alert after receiving information about a potential "living threat."

Is the security team finally admitting that the Living Avenger is running rampant through the underworld?

Speaking with Mann Down earlier this evening, newly appointed Security Commissioner, Stephen Kennedy, refused to comment, instead urging the public to remain calm but vigilant. "We have stationed guards at all streams and ports of entry into and out of the underworld for the next four days," he said.

Cora sank to the floor. "I can't stay here for four days!"

"Actually you can't stay here for more than—"

Before Euri could finish the sentence, Jack shot her a fierce look. Cora looked frantic enough as it was. If she found out that they would automatically be dead after more than three days in the underworld, she would really panic.

"For more than what?" asked Cora.

"Euri means we can't stay in this apartment for more than a few hours," Jack hastily explained. "We should go somewhere else." Jack silently reread the headline and turned to Euri. "What happened to Clubber?"

Clubber Williams was the old head of the guards. During Jack's last visit to the underworld, Clubber had tried to kill Jack by tossing him out a fourth-story window.

"They fired him for unprofessional conduct," said Euri. "And for not catching you. Kennedy was the city's police commissioner in the 1950s—he cracked down on juvenile delinquents."

"Who's the Living Avenger?" Cora asked.

"Um, I think that might be me," Jack said. He tried to give Cora a reassuring smile, but she was busy frantically pressing buttons on her cell phone.

"Neat name," said Euri. "Do you have a mask, too?"

"Very funny."

"Enjoy this double destruction," the man screeched while strumming his restrung guitar. Jack felt like cutting the guitar strings himself.

Cora finally gave up on her phone. "I don't even know what time it is!"

Jack pulled Dylan Thomas's watch out of his pocket and tipped the face so Cora could see it. "If you take a watch into the underworld it will stop working, but this one is from here. It's almost eleven."

Cora waved it away. "I'm supposed to be home by now. My mom is going to freak!"

The man stopped playing and leaned his chin on the top of his guitar, as if Cora's despair had spread to him.

"It'll be okay," Jack stuttered. "Look, I'm sure it will be. There must be another way out that the guards don't know about."

"But you said we had to go back to the living world the way we came," Cora said.

"We know there's at least one secret way back that allows you to break the rule," said Jack. "I took it last time. And if there's one, there must be more. Right, Euri?"

He hoped Euri would say something positive, but she just shrugged. "You mean that storm drain you tried to take me out last time? The guards are all over that now."

Cora stood up and grabbed Jack's arm. "You've got to take me home."

"I will," said Jack soothingly. "We'll figure it out."

"No, I mean right now." Cora's voice began to rise as she tightened her grip around his arm. Jack had never seen her like this. "I need to see my mom *right now!*" she repeated.

"You're wasting your time," said Euri. "Your mom won't be able to see—"

"I'll go myself!" Cora interrupted. "I'll walk." She ran to the window, opened it with a bang, and climbed out onto the fire escape.

"Wait!" Jack called after her. "I'll take you."

"You're making a big mistake," said Euri.

Jack cast a sorrowful glance back at her. "I already did." He flew through the window after Cora.

XI | A Living Ghost

As they shot up off the fire escape and over the tenement roofs, Euri flying alongside them, Cora gave him terse directions. "FDR Drive, north."

"You live on the Upper East Side?" asked Euri. To Jack's relief, her tone was friendly for the first time since she'd met Cora. As they joined the aerial highway of ghosts zooming uptown over the red brake lights of cars below, she added, "That's where I grew up. On Fifth, across from the park. Where are you?"

Cora didn't answer. She seemed so preoccupied that she didn't even flinch as they flew perilously close to an obese ghost in a caftan. They darted past a restaurant that was perched on the East River, and through a midtown tunnel, where they flew inches above the yellow roofs of taxis. They sailed right past the Upper East Side.

"Get off at 106th," Cora ordered curtly.

Jack obediently turned off the highway above the next exit ramp. They passed a cluster of high-rise projects then flew west past low-slung brick storefronts advertising dentists, unisex barbers, and lawyers in both Spanish and English. At Lexington Avenue, Cora directed them north. Music drifted from open apartment windows and, in the orange glow of the streetlights, Jack could see colorful murals painted on the walls of the stores and community centers—sad-eyed saints, Puerto Rican flags, lines of poetry.

"Stop," said Cora curtly, at the corner of 110th street. "I'm right here." She pointed to a half-open window directly above a convenience store that was papered in beer and cigarette ads.

Euri raised an eyebrow. "This is where you live?"

Cora glared at her. "What's wrong with it?"

Jack thought of the other students at Chapman, how so many of them lived in fancy buildings on Central Park West like Austin, or in Fifth Avenue penthouses like Euri once did. In an instant, he understood why Cora had never invited anyone over. "Nothing is wrong," he said quickly. "Let's go find your mom."

"Bad idea," Euri mouthed.

He flew Cora over to the window and pulled her through it. Euri floated after them. Inside, it was warm and a fan whirred noisily overhead. The room was small but neat, with a TV, several potted plants resting on crocheted doilies, a red velvet sofa, and a calendar of saints. On a side table was a framed photo of a chubby, dark-haired child in a white dress, clutching a bouquet in front of a fake backdrop of a field. HIJA was engraved atop it. Next to the photo, Jack noticed a basket stacked high with prescription bottles.

"Mama!" Cora shouted.

From another part of the apartment, they heard a plaintive voice. "Cora, Cora, Cora. *¿Dónde estás tú?*"

"I'm here," Cora shouted, running into the other room.

Jack and Euri followed her through a sweet-smelling kitchen and into a bedroom where a small woman with short, dark hair and Cora's round face sat in a wheelchair, staring anxiously at a cell phone. Jack suddenly realized that he wasn't the only one with secrets. Cora had never told him that her mother was in a wheelchair. He had been so worried about what she thought of him that he had never really thought about what her life was like. But then he remembered all the calls from her mother, how she was always hurrying home, even the reason she'd given for why she would never commit suicide.

"Mama!" Cora shouted, but her mother didn't look up. Cora knelt in front of her, and rested her head in her mother's lap. "*Estoy bien, Mama,*" she said. "*Estoy bien.*"

But her mother's hand passed right through Cora's head as she adjusted her skirt. After a deep sigh, she looked back at the phone.

Cora turned to face Jack. Her eyes were wet. "Why can't she hear me?"

"Because we're in the underworld—" he started to explain.

"She's got to know I'm here!" Cora interrupted. "Mama," she said, peering into her mother's eyes. "Look at me!"

But her mother wheeled through her to the window and looked out.

Cora began to cry. "I can't leave her alone."

Jack wanted to comfort her, but he didn't know what to say. He reached out his hand, then let it fall back to his side. "I didn't know she was—" He pointed to the wheelchair.

"I don't tell most people," Cora snapped. "She has this muscle disease. It's not a big deal. She's only needed the wheelchair for a couple years. But I can't leave her alone. I need to stay."

"This is ridiculous," said Euri.

They both turned to look at her.

"You're right," she continued, mimicking Cora's outraged stare. "You should stay here for eternity."

Cora's mouth twitched. "What do you know? You didn't even get along with your parents!"

Euri shot a hard glance at Jack, which he ignored. "Your mom's sick," she said to Cora, "but she can survive without you. You need to take care of yourself."

Cora shook her head vehemently. "No way. She can't. Not for four whole days."

Euri started to speak, but Jack cut her off. "I'll make sure we find a way out before then," he said. He tried to sound confident, but he had absolutely no idea what to do next. He should never have dragged her into the underworld just to show off his powers. Euri was right. A freak like him belonged here, but not Cora.

"We both will," added Euri.

Jack looked at her, surprised by her offer, but she just shrugged. He figured she felt sorry for Cora. "You shouldn't panic," he told Cora.

"Not yet, anyway," said Euri. "Besides, isn't there someone who can help her?"

Cora took a deep breath. "I guess she can call the neighbor. And I made her some meals yesterday."

"She's going to be okay," said Euri.

"You could have told me about her," Jack said quietly. "I would have understood."

"I don't want people feeling sorry for me," said Cora. "Ellen knows, but that's it."

Jack thought about how he, too, dreaded people finding out about his mother and feeling sorry for him. Cora seemed even more amazing to him, being on scholarship, taking care of her mother, and still acting as fearless and confident as she did at Chapman. It was her crush on Austin that made her seem ordinary. But he could never tell her that.

As he gently led Cora to the window, she looked back over her shoulder at her mom. "I'll be back soon," she whispered. "*Te quiero.*"

They flew up onto the tar roof of the building. Cora fixed Jack and Euri with a determined look and took out a stick of gum. "I want to know every possible way we can get out of here."

But before she could unwrap it, Jack grabbed the stick of gum from her and tossed it off the roof.

"What are you doing? I only have three pieces left!"

"You can't eat in the underworld. It's like the Proserpina myth."

"Is chewing gum eating?" Cora asked.

"I wouldn't risk it," said Euri.

"Well, I need to think," said Cora. She pretended to put a piece of gum in her mouth and started to chew.

Jack opened his backpack and pulled out the Viele map with its squiggles of rivers and faded city grid. "Last time I was here, my mother told us about a secret way out of the underworld on this map. The guards know about it now, but there may be other hidden exits that they don't know about."

"Trouble is," said Euri, "your mom has moved on.

We need to find someone else who would know where they are."

Cora hunched over the map. "It says it was prepared by someone named Egbert Viele."

Jack brightened. "Viele was a city engineer in the nineteenth century. He knew everything about the city's secret water sources. If there's a secret way out, he'll know it."

"Good," said Cora, pretending to blow a bubble. "How do we find him?"

"It's easy," said Jack, growing excited as he spoke. "There are death records for everyone in the underworld. You can look anyone up by the year they died and the death record will tell you where they haunt. Once we find out Viele's haunt, then we'll just go there and ask him if there are any other ways out. Other secret rivers or streams."

"How about if he's moved on?" Euri asked.

"Well, then we'll figure something else out." He turned to Cora. "The death record tells you whether someone has moved on or not, too. If they've moved on, there is a stamp of a bridge."

"There certainly seem to be a lot of ghosts here who haven't moved on yet—" Cora said.

"Who don't want to," interrupted Euri fiercely.

"I say we do it," said Cora. "Where are the death records kept?"

"There are different keepers for each year," said Jack. "You just have to ask around."

A knowing smile spread across Euri's pale face. "I know just the person who can help."

XII | Kore

Jack wasn't surprised when Euri touched down on a set of stairs rising in between a pair of stone lions. In front of them were the grand arches and Roman columns of the New York Public Library. "You're taking us to see Professor Schmitt," Jack guessed.

"Exactly," said Euri. "He was alive at the same time as Viele, and he knows the map. He'll definitely know who has his death record."

"Who's Professor Schmitt?" asked Cora.

"Euri's French tutor," said Jack. "He was the one who explained to us who Viele was in the first place."

Euri's face softened as she added, "I haven't seen him since I got sent to Bloomingdale." She eagerly began to fly up the steps toward one of the padlocked bronze front doors. Cora instinctively closed her eyes as they floated through the door after her.

They passed into an echoing marble hall lit by a blaze of electric candles. Just as Jack remembered from his last visit, there were ghosts everywhere: they flew up the sweeping double staircases laden with books, hung from the chandeliers reading yellowed newspapers, and floated through the air arguing about the meaning of a text. "I guess you can get a lot of reading done after you're dead," Cora observed.

"Reading is the number one afterlife activity," boasted a ghost with a big Adam's apple and a bow tie behind the reference desk. "Now, if you'll please just sign in."

"Sign in?" said Euri. "I've never had to sign in before."

"It's part of the new security measures," replied the librarian. "It'll just take a moment." He held out a stubby pencil and a clipboard.

Euri looked at the clipboard, shrugged, and wrote, *S. O' Hara.* Then, with a wink, she passed the clipboard to Cora.

Cora hesitated and then quickly wrote, *Dorothy Gale.*

Jack took the clipboard but before he could write down a name, a tall, thick-necked guard blew in through the wall behind the reception desk and nodded sternly at the librarian. Jack froze.

"I'm afraid you've been randomly selected for an interview with a member of the Underworld Security Team," said the librarian to Jack. "I'm sorry. This will just take a moment."

Jack hesitated. If he grabbed Cora and flew away now,

the guards would be on to them. But perhaps they already were and had set up this trap for him, hoping to get him alone so they could feed him to Cerberus. Jack gave a quick glance behind him. Euri, he noticed, had grabbed Cora's hand and was floating slowly back away from the reception desk. No one seemed to be stopping them. There were no signs of Cerberus either. "Um, okay," he said.

The guard directed Jack to follow him across the hall and into what appeared to be a coat-check room. Jack was relieved to discover it was empty, and there were no other guards inside. "You can just float right there," the guard said in a gruff New York accent, pointing to the attendant's chair.

As Jack hovered stiffly above the chair, the guard grabbed a pencil in his thick hands and slowly began to fill out some paperwork. "The new head of the security team likes everything in writing," he explained.

"He sounds thorough," said Jack politely.

"He's a thorough pain in the—" The guard caught himself. "So what's your name, kid?"

"Holden Caulfield," blurted Jack.

"And why are you haunting the library, Mr. Cauliflower?"

"I'm visiting a friend who haunts the library," Jack said, trying to be as honest as possible.

"How long have you been dead?"

"Two days," Jack lied.

The guard peered at him skeptically.

"Well, really less than that," Jack stuttered.

"You look more dead than two days," said the guard.

For a moment, Jack forgot himself. "I look *more* dead?"

The guard ignored him and began to read from a card. "Answer the following questions yes or no. Have you noticed any suspicious persons or groups on your fountain commute?"

"No," Jack said. Why did he look so dead?

"Has anyone asked you to find a death record for them or hold their hand as they fly?" the guard read.

"No," Jack lied.

"Have you ever engaged in an illegal activity such as, but not limited to, the use of Ouija boards or other paranormal enhancers?"

"Never," said Jack, shaking his head furiously for effect. "But what does that have to do with the security alert?"

The guard pointed to an official-looking letter taped to the wall. NEW UNDERWORLD SECURITY FORCE GUIDELINES FROM COMMISSIONER STEPHEN KENNEDY. APPLY THE LAW AND APPLY IT VIGOROUSLY!

"We're cracking down on the smaller crimes that lead to larger ones," the guard explained. "There are harsher penalties, too. The new commissioner doesn't believe in therapy. He believes in jail." The guard snickered. "The Living Avenger is going to rot there!"

"Am I done?" squeaked Jack.

"Yeah," said the guard, with a wave of his hand. He seemed preoccupied as he filled out the last of his paperwork. Jack flew away slowly so as not to arouse suspicion. As soon as he left the coat-check room, Euri flew up to him. "I was just about to go in there!"

"I'm fine," said Jack. He scanned the hall. "Where's Cora?"

"There was a 'Now That You're Dead' seminar going on upstairs. I figured she'd be safe there."

On his last trip, Euri had taken him to the introductory seminar for new ghosts. Jack had found it mostly useful except for regulation 41.5a, which explained what Cerberus did to living intruders. But Cora already knew that. "She might as well hear the rules of the underworld," he said with a sigh. "We may never get out."

Euri gave him a curious look. "What did that guard tell you?"

"They're looking for us—or me, at least."

"Professor Schmitt will help."

Jack nodded, trying to feel reassured.

"Come on," said Euri. "Let's get Cora."

They flew up one of the sweeping staircases to the

McGraw Rotunda, where a motley group of ghosts was standing under Euri's favorite mural—the Greek god Prometheus giving the knowledge of fire to mankind. Through invisible stereos, Jack could hear the fading strains of classical music. The seminar, Jack guessed, had just ended.

"You're okay," said Cora with a deep breath when she spotted Jack.

"Let's go," said Euri impatiently. Dragging both of them along, she flew into the catalog room, then through another door and a foyer into the reading room. Just as it had been on his last visit to the underworld, the reading room was packed with ghosts hovering beside the sturdy wooden tables as they paged through books, and floating under the enormous mural of a cloud-dappled sky on the ceiling, pretending to sun themselves. Euri flew to the back of the room and scanned the long wooden tables in the back. "Where is he?"

They flew slowly around the room, dodging ghost librarians who flew out from the shelves on the balcony balancing teetering stacks of books. "I'm sure that's his table," Euri said, pointing to one in the middle of the room. She floated down to it and tapped the shoulder of a ghost hunched over a book. But as soon as the ghost straightened up, Jack realized he wasn't Professor Schmitt but a man with a flop of graying brown hair and the wrinkled face of a prune, who was furiously crossing something out on a page of the book in his hand. "Yes?" he asked in a British accent.

"You're not . . ." Euri started to say. "I'm looking for an older ghost. His name is Professor Schmitt. Have you seen him?"

The ghost brightened. "The translator? He was a hunchback, yes?"

Jack nodded. "That's him."

The ghost gestured toward an empty spot at the table. "He moved on just a few weeks ago," he said. Then he opened an identical book to the same page and resumed scribbling.

Jack tried to hide his mounting panic. What were they going to do now? He turned to Euri. But she was staring at Professor Schmitt's empty seat, blinking back tears.

"I'm sorry," Jack said.

"It's no big deal," said Euri in a flat voice. "He was just someone to practice French with."

Before Jack could comfort her, she flew to the other side of the table and flopped into Professor Schmitt's empty chair.

Jack looked at Cora. She was chewing intently on a lock of her hair. "We have to start with what we know," she finally said.

"What do you mean?" Jack asked.

"Like when you do a tough crossword, you're supposed to start with what you know. We know Viele made maps. Perhaps the library has a map room?"

"It certainly does," said the ghost with the flop of hair and the wrinkled face.

Jack turned around to stare at him. He looked familiar.

"I love maps," he continued, opening a third copy of the book and brandishing a pen. "Particularly of Iceland. It's my favorite country."

"What are you doing to those books?" Jack asked.

"Unfortunately, I can't truly alter them," said the ghost, holding up his pen with a sigh. "It's invisible ink— at least to the living." He turned the spine toward Jack so he could see the title, *The Collected Poetry of W. H. Auden*. "This poem 'September 1, 1939,' " he said, pointing at the pages he had tampered with. "It's rubbish."

"No, it's not!" said Cora. "We read it in class."

Jack nodded enthusiastically. "It's a great poem. 'We must love one another or die,' " he quoted.

The ghost gave a pained look. "Exactly! What a stupid line. It's not a choice. Even if we love one another, we're going to die anyway."

"Well, maybe the poet disagrees," said Jack defensively.

"I don't think so," said the ghost. "I am the poet."

"Auden?"

"We must love one another *and* die," Auden continued, shaking his head. "That's the way the line should read. There's only one choice. We must love one another despite death, rejection, loneliness—not because love will save us from these things."

"What's the point of love, then?" Jack asked.

The poet grinned. "There is no point. And you are . . . ?"

"Jack."

Cora held out her hand. "Cora."

The poet nodded at Jack and then clasped Cora's hand in his large ones. "A variant of *Kore*, the Greek word for 'maiden.' Also, an old Greek name for Proserpina. Make sure you don't eat anything while you're here, my dear."

Cora shifted uneasily. "But my mother named me for the Spanish word for 'heart,' *Corazón*."

"And she's going to get back to her mother," Jack blurted out. "I'm going to make sure she does."

The poet looked from Cora to Jack. "So you are both stranded here?"

Jack looked down, ashamed of the mess he had made. He thought of the story of Proserpina in the *Metamorphoses* and suddenly felt sorry for Pluto. If he hadn't had a crush, he wouldn't have dragged *his* Kore into the underworld just as Jack had done.

"What map are you looking for?" asked Auden.

"We're not looking for a map exactly," said Jack. "We're looking for a mapmaker. Egbert Viele." He pulled out the map of the underground streams and rivers. "He made this. We're searching for his death record."

"Before my time, I'm afraid. But," he added with a wink, "I have an in with the map-room librarian. Come, I'll take you there."

Jack waved Euri over. "This is the poet Auden," he explained. "He's going to take us to the map room."

But Euri just picked at her skirt.

"I'm sorry about your friend," Auden said to her as they floated out of the reading room and back down the stairs. "I can tell you cared deeply for him."

"I don't care for anyone," she shot back.

"'If equal affection cannot be,'" said Auden, "'Let the more loving one be me.'"

Jack recognized the lines. They were from another of Auden's poems.

But Euri looked unmoved. "No offense," she said. "But I only like Donne."

"A fine poet," Auden said generously.

They followed the poet back downstairs into a small, square room that reminded Jack of the inside of a music box, with a gold painted ceiling and four golden chandeliers. The walls were lined with old maps of the world, and even the face of the clock, Jack noticed, was a map. Auden led them to the information desk.

"Hello, Oscar," he said to a ghost dressed in a

nightshirt and sporting a wiry mustache. "I'd like to take a look at the Kjartansson map of Iceland. And these young-sters are looking for . . ."

"The death record for Egbert Viele," said Jack.

Oscar raised an eyebrow. "I'm not really supposed to give out death record information without getting permission first from the guards. Part of the new security regulations."

"Do it for me, won't you, Oscar?" said the poet in a soothing voice.

The librarian shifted his eyes around the map room. When he seemed satisfied that no one was watching, he shuffled through a card catalog, stopping on an entry. Then he jotted something down on a piece of paper and slid it to Jack. "Egbert Ludovicus Viele, June 17, 1825-April 22, 1902," it read. "Contact Washington Irving Bishop, 1902 death record keeper, Lamb's Theater."

XIII | Eleanor Fletcher Bishop

It was just after two when Jack, holding tight to Cora's hand, touched down behind Euri on a small Midtown block of Korean restaurants and private clubs between Sixth and Seventh Avenues.

"I think it's in here," Euri said, pointing to an elegant six-story stone and brick building with a small maroon awning. A living woman with blue hair tucked under a plaid cap walked by with her companion. Pointing to the theater, she began to talk in an animated voice about— Jack couldn't be sure—but what sounded like the musical *Cats*.

"Is that still on Broadway?" Cora asked.

"We're not on Broadway," sniffed Euri. "This is *Off-Broadway*."

Jack tried to smile at her, but she refused to look at him. "I guess that's why this doesn't look like much of a theater," he said, remembering the flashy marquee and large crowds spilling onto the street at the St. James, the last Broadway theater they had visited. He pulled Cora through the door and into a deserted lobby that reminded Jack of a small, third-rate hotel. There was an unmanned front desk with paper signs taped to the front of it. MANHATTAN CHURCH OF THE NAZARENE SERVICE, read the first; SUNDAY 11 A.M., THIRD FLOOR. The second read, MOSCOW CATS THEATER. SATURDAY 8 P.M., THIRD FLOOR. But it was the third that caught Jack's attention. It read, WASHINGTON IRVING BISHOP next to a big hieroglyphic Egyptian eye. SATURDAY MIDNIGHT, THIRD FLOOR.

"Bingo," said Jack.

"Let's go," said Euri, floating up till her head disappeared through the ceiling.

Cora looked anxiously at Euri's dangling, disembodied legs. "Would you mind if we take the elevator?"

Jack gave a sympathetic smile. "Sure." He quickly flew up, grabbed Euri's foot, and pulled her back down through the ceiling.

"What are you doing?" she asked.

"Let's take the elevator."

Euri looked at Cora and with a shake of her head, hit the call button. A few seconds later, with a clatter, it opened. Even Euri leaped backward as a snub-nosed living man with smears of greasepaint still on his face appeared in front of them, balancing several cages. As they stepped through him to get on the elevator, cries and yowls began to echo from the cages and through the empty lobby. *"Teehuh,"* the man purred back at them in a language that Jack guessed must be Russian.

"The cast of *Cats,*" said Euri dryly. "I hear they don't give autographs, though."

For the first time since she had realized they were trapped in the underworld, Cora laughed. Euri began to grin but then looked annoyed. "It wasn't that funny," she grumbled.

The elevator doors opened with a creak, and they floated out and through a set of wooden doors into a small, darkened, wood-paneled theater. A bearded man in a tuxedo was standing silently on an empty stage with a blindfold over his eyes. An audience of ghosts in nineteenth-century waistcoats and dresses floated above the folding seats, watching him intently. "Riveting show," said Euri.

"Quiet!" interrupted a large ghost wearing a long black dress and lacy black veil. "Sir Washington Irving Bishop is about to perform the astounding blindfold fly trick!"

"That's Washington Irving Bishop?" Jack asked.

"The one and only," said the woman. "The king of mentalists, mind-readers, and magicians. The international sensation! Back once again after his unforgettable 1889 show!" She pulled a handkerchief out of her pocket and, as if overcome by her own words, blew her nose.

"What's the blindfold fly trick?" Cora asked.

"It's the most remarkable trick ever," the woman in black confided. "Sir Washington Irving Bishop will fly around the theater blindfolded, using nothing but the powers of his mind to stop him from crashing into things. Watch!"

Jack obediently turned to the stage where the magician had begun to float up over the crowd and was heading perilously toward the railing of the balcony. Just as the woman in black gasped in horror, the magician began to float away from the balcony. The crowd murmured. Even Jack was impressed until Euri quipped, "He's a ghost. He could just go through it."

But as the man headed straight for a bank of lights, the audience craned their necks anxiously. "Amazing!" shrieked the woman in black as the magician once again turned. Several ghosts in the audience began to applaud.

"There's something funny going on here," said Euri.

"How could you say that?" demanded the woman, who quickly turned to watch the magician and gasped again as he just barely avoided crashing into one side of the stage.

"You're cuing him," Euri said. "Every time he almost hits something, you gasp or say 'amazing.'"

The woman leaned over Euri in a menacing way. "How dare you! Sir Washington Irving Bishop has powers from the beyond!"

"This *is* the beyond," said Euri.

Jack tapped the woman's sleeve. "Um, he's about to hit that piano."

"Amazing!" the woman shrieked. Turning back to Euri, she narrowed her eyes. "You must be here from a competing act. Anna Eva Fay! Or J. N. Maskelyne. You're wasting your time. No mentalist is as great as Sir Washington Irving Bishop!"

"We're not here from a competing act," Cora said soothingly. "We just want to talk to him about some death records. . . ."

"Are you his manager?" Jack asked. "Maybe you can introduce us after the show?"

"His manager?" The woman glowered. "I'm his mother!"

"He's about to crash into that row of seats," said Cora.

Euri gasped.

The woman in black gave her a dirty look. "I had that one." Then she turned back to Jack. "I doubt a personage as important as Washington Irving Bishop has time to discuss death records with you."

Jack opened his mouth to protest, but Cora caught his eye and shook her head. "Mrs. Bishop, your son seems very talented," she said brightly. "What was his unforget-table 1889 show?"

Washington Irving Bishop's mother woefully draped an arm across her forehead. "Butchery!" she wailed.

"The flair for drama runs in the family," whispered Euri.

"Butchery?" Cora repeated. "I'm not familiar with that trick. . . ."

"Amazing!" Euri shouted, preventing the magician from colliding with the ceiling.

Washington Irving Bishop's mother reached beneath one of the theater seats and pulled out a book that she handed to Cora. "My great opus," she explained. Jack and Euri leaned over Cora's shoulder to read its title: *A Mother's Life Dedicated and an Appeal for Justice to All Brother Masons and the General Public; A Synopsis of the Butchery of the Late Sir Washington Irving Bishop. By Eleanor Fletcher Bishop.*

"Something tells me this isn't a beach read," said Euri.

Eleanor Fletcher Bishop ignored this comment and reaching over Cora, opened the book to a frontispiece photograph. "And there I am in maternal anguish," she said, pointing to a woman decked out entirely in black leaning over Washington Irving Bishop's casket and star-ing lovingly at a line around the top of his forehead.

"What happened to him?" Cora asked.

Euri gasped and the magician narrowly missed the light fixture.

Eleanor Fletcher Bishop wrung her hands. "In the middle of his show at the Lambs Theatrical Club's 26th Street location, he had a fainting spell. He was prone to them, which is why I always left a note in his pocket cautioning not to bury him even if he seemed dead. Some doctors were in the audience that night, however, and they didn't read the note. His pulse was so weak, they assumed he had died, and so," Eleanor Fletcher Bishop let out a loud sob, "they autopsied him alive!"

"That's horrible!" said Cora.

"Yes it is!" declared Eleanor Fletcher Bishop.

"Amazing!" shouted Euri. Only Jack, however, noticed that the magician was not in danger of hitting anything. Euri was just having fun sending him in different directions.

"Since then he has re-enacted his heart-stopping show at past and present locations of the Lambs Club, although this one is by far our favorite." Eleanor Fletcher Bishop looked kindly at Cora. "Who do you want to find in the 1902 records, my dear?"

"Viele," said Cora. "Egbert Viele."

"The water engineer," added Jack.

Ignoring her son spinning in helpless circles above her, Eleanor Fletcher Bishop continued in a loud whisper,

"Well, I've certainly heard of him. Wretched man. He sued just about everyone. Here." She reached under her seat, pulled out a black leather-bound book, and gave it to Cora. "My son should find a nice young ghost like you," she said with a sigh.

"I thought Washington Irving Bishop kept the records," said Jack as Cora handed it to him.

"Are you kidding?" said Mrs. Bishop. "He's a nincompoop. Look at him!"

Washington Irving Bishop was jerking around over the increasingly confused audience as Euri gasped over and over in quick succession. Jack turned back to the little black book. He stared at the cover, afraid to open it. What would they do if Viele had already moved on?

"What does it say?" asked Euri, taking a break between gasps.

Cora leaned closer as Jack flipped through it—Cs, Ls, Os—till he reached the Vs. Valmont, Van Dyne, Velasquez. "Viele!" Jack said, pointing to a name at the top of the page. He ran his finger along the column beside it. There was no bridge. He took a deep breath. Everything would be okay. Viele hadn't moved on.

But then, with a sinking feeling, Jack noticed Viele's haunts column. It was empty save for an official-looking stamp that read UNDISCLOSED LOCATION: HAUNT CLASSIFIED.

XIV | Tunnel Number Three

"Haunt classified?" Cora read aloud. "What does that mean?"

"It means we just hit a dead end," said Euri.

Jack gave her a funny look.

Euri shrugged. "Okay, wrong choice of words. But there is an upside."

"This better be good," said Cora.

"Jack's theory about Viele being the one ghost who can help us find a way out must be right. Why else would the guards classify his haunt? They don't want him found."

Cora frowned and shook her head. "Then we've got to figure out a way to find him. I can't stay here four nights!"

Jack looked around to make sure no ghosts besides Euri had heard her. Luckily, Mrs. Bishop was busy trying to regain control of Washington Irving Bishop, who had stopped following her cues.

"We've got to try to figure out where he would haunt,

by ourselves," Cora continued. "Euri, how do ghosts pick their haunts?"

"They usually haunt places where they spent a lot of time when they were alive."

"And tell me again what we know about Viele's life?"

Jack pulled out the map. "He made this map of all the water sources in Manhattan."

"So maybe he haunts someplace that has to do with water?"

"That could be anywhere," said Euri. "Manhattan is surrounded by water. And there are hundreds of streams and pipes and sewers."

Jack shook his head. "But Viele's map is concerned with only one type of water. Drinking water. He wanted to make sure builders wouldn't build on top of underground streams and contaminate them," said Jack, remembering what Professor Schmitt had told him.

Cora turned to Euri. "If you cared about the city's drinking water, where would you haunt?"

Euri began to roll her eyes but then suddenly stopped. "Wait," she said as her lips curled into a smile, "it totally makes sense. Tunnel Number Three!"

It was nearly 5 A.M., just two hours to sunrise, when Jack, Cora, and Euri touched down at the intersection of Tenth Avenue and 31st Street. At the northwest corner of Tenth Avenue, Jack spotted a tall aluminum fence. Orange warning signs nailed to the top of the fence read:

1 LONG WHISTLE, THREE MINUTES TO BLAST.

2 SHORT WHISTLES, ONE MINUTE TO BLAST.

3 LONG WHISTLES, ALL CLEAR.

"Where are we?"

"That's the entrance to the tunnel," Euri explained.

They flew over the fence and joined a group of living men in hard hats and steel-tipped rubber boots who stood around an enormous hole, eating sandwiches and smoking. Suddenly, with a whirring sound, a giant winch suspended over the hole dragged a green metal cage to the surface, and the men stamped out their cigarettes and crumpled the aluminum foil around their sandwiches into their pockets. Then one of them opened the door of the cage and the rest quietly boarded. The door of the cage slammed shut, and with a creak of cable, it began to descend into the hole.

"What *is* Tunnel Number Three, exactly?" said Cora, peering down into the dark hole after the cage.

"It's a water tunnel the city has been building for decades," Euri explained. "I once went into it—" She cleared her throat. "It was before I discovered the cockroaches. Anyway, if Viele still cares about drinking water, it's the logical place for him to haunt. There are two other water tunnels under the city that bring in water from upstate. But they're on the verge of falling apart, and so, for the last twenty years, they've been rushing to build this one."

"How do we get down there?" asked Cora.

Euri grabbed Cora's hand. "Three, two . . ." she began to count down.

Cora's eyes widened. "You've got to be kidding."

"One!" shouted Euri as she dove headfirst into the hole, pulling Cora with her.

Jack quickly lost sight of them, but Cora's screams echoed back out of the darkness. "Wait up!" he yelled, jumping in after them.

As Jack fell, the light from the surface began to shrink. He sailed through the cage where the workers were crammed together, their pale faces alert, and past walls of dripping black rock. He slowed himself down and peered beneath him, but he could only see darkness, no bottom to the enormous hole. He was sure that he had already fallen hundreds of feet, but it didn't seem possible to travel this far down in the middle of Manhattan.

Looking up, the hole to the surface had become a pin-prick of faint light. The air grew warmer as he floated down, and drops of chemical-smelling water splashed against his face. Voices began to echo up from an invisible bottom, and fiery sparks burst out of the darkness. Jack landed in a puddle of icy water. Mist blanketed the air and he struggled to get his bearing. As he looked around, he caught glimpses of electric bulbs hanging from wires, rock walls buttressed with steel, and flashlights fading in and out of the mist, like ships caught in fog. A shape moved toward him and he suddenly realized it was Cora. Her hair was standing on end so she almost looked like a ghost herself. Euri floated next to her, grinning.

"Are you all right?" Jack asked.

"Do I look all right?" Cora answered.

"This ain't a playground," said a deep voice with a thick New York accent.

Jack turned. A barrel-chested ghost in a yellow slicker was staring at him with his arms crossed over his chest. "The way you kids hurled yourselves down here . . . ya coulda killed me."

"But you're already dead," said Euri.

"And you know what killed me?" the man continued angrily.

"A falling ghost?" said Euri.

"An icicle. It fell off the top of the winch at the surface."

Jack couldn't help himself. "You were impaled by an icicle?"

"You ever see an icicle fall five hundred feet? It becomes a weapon. But sandhogs have had worse deaths. Jimmy over there was cut in two by a drill." He pointed to another slicker-clad ghost who was inspecting a case of dynamite.

Cora shuddered. "We'll be more careful. We've actually come looking for someone."

"A hog?" the man interrupted.

Jack gave him a confused look.

"That's what we're called—the men that work these tunnels—sandhogs."

"No," said Jack. "An engineer. Egbert Viele."

A loud roar suddenly filled the bottom of the tunnel. Jack and Cora jumped.

The ghost sandhog didn't flinch. "They're just blasting. Viele. Yeah. That guy."

"See, he's down here!" Jack whispered to Cora.

"A real know-it-all," the sandhog continued with a dismissive look. "He used to haunt over by the mole."

Cora's face fell. "Used to?"

"He stopped coming here a few months ago."

"Do you know where he went?" Jack asked.

The hog shrugged. "No idea. He left a few things by the mole, though."

"Where's . . . the mole?" said Cora.

"That's the big drill. Come on. I'll show you."

The sandhog ghost floated over the flooded shaft, down a tunnel lined with ventilation pipes, and hopped onto a railroad car. "This is almost as fast as flying," he explained. Jack, Euri, and Cora boarded the back of the car. As it rattled through the tunnel, they passed living men with dirt-stained faces, shaking with their drills as they bored into rocks, and other living men piling debris onto conveyer belts. Finally, the car stopped in front of a giant steel machine that took up the entire diameter of the tunnel. Two living sandhogs were wedged inside of it while several more dead ones were wedged behind them.

"Hey, Clancy!" their guide shouted. "I have a bunch of kids here that was looking for Viele. They want to see the stuff he left behind."

A red-faced ghost with a large belly backed out of the drill and surveyed them. He pointed to Cora. "Jeez, kid, you almost look alive."

"They just took her off life support a few hours ago," said Euri. "We're looking for anything Viele left behind."

Clancy floated over to an indentation in the rock on one side of the tunnel that Jack hadn't noticed before. "He used to show up here every night, like this was his office or something," Clancy explained. "Bossy fellow. He was always shouting at the living hogs about making sure the mole didn't hit a spring. Like they could hear him."

"Do you know where he went?" Cora asked.

"He didn't talk to us much. Before he left we asked him where he was going, and he just smiled. Said that he was going someplace with a beautiful view." Clancy looked around appreciatively at the wet, shining walls and patches of mist and shook his head. "He had a perfectly good one right here." He reached into his pocket, pulled out a sheaf of papers, and handed them to Jack. "Anyway, here's what he left behind. Take what you like." A whirring sound filled the tunnel as a living hog switched on a rotor on the mole. "I'd better go."

With a grinding roar, the drill began to grind into the bedrock, shaking the entire tunnel.

"A beautiful view? Do you think he's moved on?" Cora shouted over the din.

"The record would have said that," Euri shouted back. "Not 'haunt classified.'"

"Maybe he just wanted to get out of here," yelled Jack over the earsplitting noise. He began floating away from the mole and back out of the tunnel. "Come on. We can look at these aboveground."

As they rose up out of Tunnel Number Three, the sound of drilling and the orange sparks faded below. They flew through an ascending cage full of living men, their faces black with dust, their eerily white eyeballs staring anxiously upward. The entrance to the tunnel grew from a pinprick to a manhole to a small, pale pool of night sky. At last, they were out, and Jack felt jarred by the relative quiet and the handful of living people hurrying by as the whistles blew, oblivious to the explosions going on beneath their feet.

They landed a couple of blocks away in front of a closed deli called the Terminal Food Shop, its neon signs advertising beef hot dogs and chicken fingers. Jack pulled out the sheaf of papers while Cora and Euri huddled around him. The first few pages were entitled "The Topology and Hydrology of New York, 1865, by Egbert L.Viele," and seemed to contain information about different water sources and whether or not they were sanitary. Then there was a copy of the water map Jack already had and another report on something called the Arcade underground railway. Finally, there was another map that Jack had never seen before. It was a small black-and-white map that showed a street grid of the middle of Manhattan interlaced with topographer's marks. MAP OF THE LANDS INCLUDED IN THE CENTRAL PARK FROM A TOPOGRAPHICAL SURVEY, JUNE 17, 1856, read lettering over the top. In the lower right-hand corner was the signature EGBERT L.VIELE.

"It's Central Park before they made Central Park," Jack remarked. He pointed to swirling patterns of lines that reminded him of fingerprints. "I think these indicate elevation."

Cora pointed to a sprinkling of neat squares in the Eighties, just east of what was marked as Eighth Avenue.

They were interspersed between what looked like rock formations. "What do you think these are?"

"I don't know," said Jack. "There is no Eighth Avenue on the Upper West Side anymore." Then he noticed something else that was no longer there. Directly east of the sprinkling of squares was a large rectangle marked RECEIVING RESERVOIR. "There's no reservoir there, either. That's the Great Lawn."

Euri looked unimpressed. "Okay, so Viele made a map of Central Park before it was Central Park. But he also made all these other reports and maps. He could be anywhere. In Central Park. At the Arcade underground railway, whatever that is. At some stream in one of these reports. If we search all the places he mentions, it could take days. And we don't have—"

Euri stopped herself just in time. But Jack knew she was right. A tossed-off remark about a beautiful view and a bunch of maps and reports didn't add up to much of a clue. He looked at his pocket watch. There was just an hour left till dawn.

"Well, we can't just give up," said Cora. "I can't stay here for four days."

Jack closed his eyes. He suddenly knew he couldn't keep on lying to Cora. He had to tell her what would happen if they didn't get out by the end of the third night. For a moment, he imagined her dead—flying alone, her once cheerful face lifeless and pale, to her mother's apartment. If she were lucky she would become a poltergeist and be able to indicate her presence the way Euri had at the tenement. But there was nothing violent about her separation from her mother, and it was more likely she'd just become an ordinary ghost, haunting her mother in the painful one-sided way that she had already done. Even worse than this image, though, was the thought of her dying on the dawn of their third night in the underworld and realizing he had lied to her.

He turned to Euri. "I need to talk to Cora alone," he said. "Is it okay if we meet you back at one of the fountains?"

Euri's face fell, but she quickly waved them off. "Fine. Meet me near the fountain at Fifty-third and Madison at dawn. I have errands to run, anyway."

XV | The Dead End

Jack flew with Cora above Lexington Avenue. It was the darkest hour of the night, just before dawn. The streets were crowded both with the dead, drifting reluctantly back to the fountains, and the living, bleary-eyed, hurrying to work or back home after the night shift. The city had finally cooled down and the sky had become overcast, the tireless lights illuminating the clouds a pinkish gray. Jack began to shoot up vertically, as if they were on an elevator racing up into the air.

"Where are we going?" Cora asked.

"I want to show you something," said Jack. First, before he told her the truth, he wanted just one more happy moment with her, the kind he had imagined having when he dragged her into the underworld in the first place.

Cora looked down in alarm. They were hundreds of feet up. Jack smiled, remembering how he had felt the same way when Euri had taken him here.

"We're almost there," he assured her, as the city shrank into a miniature kingdom below them. With a final kick of his legs, they were face-to-face with a steel eagle, and then they sailed over its head and landed on its neck. "The top of the Chrysler building," Jack explained. "It's my favorite place."

Cora had her eyes shut. She slowly opened one of them. Gradually she opened the other. The city sparkled with lights, blinking, solid, flying through the air, unmoored from the ground. To the south, rising out of a cloud, loomed the Empire State Building, the red light atop its antenna seeming to graze the sky. The wind whipped through their hair.

"Euri took me here. I didn't know I could fly then. I was pretty scared. But when I saw the view . . ."

"It's beautiful," Cora admitted. She turned to him with a serious look. "But why did you take me here? What do you want to tell me?"

Jack knew it was time. But instead, he looked out over the city. "Don't you feel like a god being up here?"

Cora frowned. "You're hiding something."

"We can only stay three days in the underworld before—" he said, half-choking on the words. "I should have told you. But I thought we'd be out by now. . . ."

"Before what?"

He opened his backpack and pulled out the *Unofficial*

Guide, flipping to the page that explained the one rule about visiting the underworld that he hadn't told her about—and that couldn't be broken. "Here," he said, handing her the guide.

Cora's eyes darted across the page as she silently read.

"I don't understand," she said a moment later. But the panic in her voice told Jack she did.

"After three days, the strain of being here becomes too much on living bodies. I should have told you."

"I'm going to die?" she said quietly.

"We still have two days," Jack said hurriedly. "We can still find Viele."

But Cora didn't seem to hear him. She grabbed his arm so hard that he felt the imprint of her fingers. "I can't die, Jack. My mother." Tears cascaded down her cheeks.

"I know," Jack said softly. "My dad . . ."

"No, you don't know!" she shouted. "She's alone here. I'm all she has." Her voice caught in her throat. She looked out over the city, but Jack could tell that the view had become to her what it had always been to Euri—a prison.

She caught his eye accusingly. "Why did you take me here?"

"I . . . I . . ." he stuttered, unable to tell her the real reason.

"You never even gave me a choice. You never told

me where we were really going. 'Magic,' you said," Cora spat out. "This isn't magic, Jack! This is death!"

"We're not dead," Jack protested. "We still have—"

"I can't believe you did this to me!" she said, cutting him off.

"I'm sorry," he whispered, barely able to speak. "I'll bring you back to your mom. I promise."

XVI | The Promise

Euri was the only ghost around by the time Jack touched down with Cora at the small cobblestone park nestled between two buildings on Fifty-third Street. The sky was turning from pinkish gray to shades of purple. Coffee carts began to arrive by the curbs, hitched to the back of beat-up station wagons, and garbage trucks rolled down the streets. Euri was floating in a ball, hugging her knees to her chest. Behind her flowed the strangest fountain that Jack had ever seen—a twenty-foot-high wall that water rushed down like a waterfall.

"There you are!" she shouted. "It's almost dawn."

"I know, I'm sorry," said Jack.

"Let's go," she snapped, flying at the watery wall and vanishing into the basin of the fountain.

Jack looked at Cora. She gazed down at the cobblestones with a grim expression. "Are you ready?" he asked as gently as he could.

"Can't we just stay up here?"

"Ghosts aren't allowed in the living world during the day."

"But I'm not a ghost," Cora said.

Once again, he had said the wrong thing. "We were counted when we came up through the fountain," he tried to explain, "so the guards would come after us if we didn't return."

Cora nodded but didn't speak. Jack flew at the wall and then felt his stomach drop as they fell with the water into the basin. He held tight to Cora's fingers as they whirled down the drain and through a series of tubes. A moment later, with a pop, they were spit out onto a dirty tunnel floor.

"Just in time," said a ghost in a nurse's uniform as she counted them in on her clicker. "Sun rises in thirty seconds."

Euri gave them an "I told you so" look, but Jack knew she wasn't really mad. "Let's go," she ordered, grabbing Jack's other hand and dragging him down the tunnel. Cora sniffed, blinking back tears, and for the first time since they'd reunited, Euri took a good look at her. "You two need some sleep," she said. "Somewhere Cerberus won't find you."

They followed her through a series of warm tunnels that sloped downward into the earth. The deeper they went, the fewer ghosts they saw. Finally, Euri stopped in front of a steel door and pressed a button on the wall next to it. A mechanical hum filled the air, and the door creaked open to reveal a metal freight elevator. "See," said Euri, looking at Cora, "we can even take the elevator down."

But Cora just shrugged.

"Down?" asked Jack. "How much farther can we go?"

"You'll see," said Euri. "No one will bother us there."

The elevator groaned as it descended. For several minutes, no one spoke. Cora looked down at her feet. Then the door creaked open, and they stepped out of it and into a steamy room nearly the size of a football field. In the center of it were what looked like enormous metal wheels with fan belts inside them. Jack couldn't believe a room of this size existed so deep underground. "Where are we?" he asked.

"Under the main concourse of Grand Central," said Euri. "This is the Dynamo Room. Very few people, living or dead, know about it. You have to really haunt the station to find it. It's not on any of the blueprints."

"Why not?" asked Jack.

"For security reasons." Euri pointed to the giant wheels. "Those big things are converters. They used to power the trains. It's a good place for you to sleep, though."

They walked past the hulking, silent converters and

floated through a glass door into a small office tucked into the back of the room. Inside was a wooden chair, a desk, and a calendar flipped to a page marked December 1989. Jack took off his sweater and gave it to Cora, who wordlessly accepted it and curled up in a corner.

"That's the worst case of mourning sickness I've ever seen," whispered Euri.

Jack also felt the bleak, hopeless feeling that all ghosts felt when they returned to the underworld after a night of haunting and remembering life. But he knew what Cora was feeling was worse than just mourning sickness. He sat down in the opposite corner of the dusty office and watched as her eyelids fluttered and her breathing became regular.

"Aren't you going to sleep, too?" asked Euri, floating above the paper-strewn desk.

"I told her the truth," Jack said. "About how we only have three nights."

"Well, that explains things," said Euri. "But why now?"

"Because I'm not sure we'll ever find Viele. I had to let her know." He rested his forehead against his knees.

Euri floated down beside him. "It's not your fault, Jack."

He lifted his head and looked at her. "You're right about me being a freak. I belong here. The guards even think I look dead. But I shouldn't have brought her."

Euri shifted uncomfortably. "I didn't really mean that."

"I'm going to get Cora back, and then maybe I'll just do what you did. Maybe I'll jump in front of a train, too."

He had barely finished when Euri grabbed him by the shoulders. Her pale eyes were fierce. "I won't ever speak to you again if you . . ." Her mouth remained open, but no words came out.

Jack suddenly felt ashamed. "I'm sorry," he said.

Euri slowly let go of his shoulders.

"I still don't understand why you jumped," Jack said quietly.

Euri said nothing, just picked at her skirt. Finally, she spoke. "I wasn't alone."

Jack turned toward her. "What do you mean?"

"When it happened. There was someone else with me. We were holding hands."

Jack wanted to ask her more, but she moved away from him and floated over to Cora. "Promise me, Jack. She goes back, you go back."

He nodded. "As long as there's still a way."

"Viele is the way. Now, get some sleep."

Jack could tell from the way that Euri somersaulted upside down and stared blankly at the wall that the conversation was over. He closed his eyes, imagining Euri standing on a train platform in Grand Central Terminal, her hand in someone else's. He had always imagined her jumping alone. Then he thought about the man she had haunted in the tenement. Was the hand she had been holding his?

XVII | Orpheus of the Lower East Side

"Wake up, Jack."

Someone was shaking his shoulder. Jack opened his eyes, a sinking feeling in his chest as he glimpsed the Dynamo Room office. He had dreamed that he and Cora were back in the living world.

Euri shook him again. "It's night. Time to get up."

"I'm awake," he said, sitting up and rubbing his eyes.

Cora sat cross-legged on the office chair staring stonily ahead. Next to her was his copy of the *Unofficial Guide*. He smiled at her, but she turned away.

"Maybe we need to take a break . . . and regroup," said Euri.

"What kind of break?" Jack asked. "We don't have much—" He looked at Cora and cut himself off.

"I need to go downtown," Euri said. "I can meet you later. . . ."

"To haunt? Now?"

Euri scowled. "I don't haunt."

"What could be more important than finding Viele and getting Cora back?" Jack snapped.

"Stop!" said Cora, surprising them both. "We don't know what to do next anyway. Let's just go with Euri."

Twenty minutes later, they shot out of a small fountain beneath a stone canopy topped with a statue of Juventas, the Roman goddess of youth. Jack could see a ring of benches and hear the squeaks of a tire swing from a playground. Past it were the four- and five-story walk-up apartments of the East Village, and he realized they were in Tompkins Square Park. It was early evening—the trees were silhouetted against a darkening-gray sky—and there were a number of living people sitting on the benches in the park or strolling through it. Jack noticed that they were wearing sweaters or jackets, and he even glimpsed an old lady in a pair of gloves and a scarf. The Indian summer was over, and he almost wondered if his abduction of Cora had caused autumn to begin.

But Cora didn't seem to notice the change in weather. She seemed tired, almost resigned. He feared that she was starting to die—in spirit, at least. As they sailed down Avenue A, over the roofs of cabs, past vintage clothing shops, dive bars, and neon diner signs, she closed her eyes.

Moments later, they landed on the familiar fire escape.

"Wait here," said Euri. Then she disappeared through the window.

Cora sat down on the fire escape and went back to reading the *Unofficial Guide*. With an impatient sigh, Jack stuck his head through the window of the tiny apartment. The musician was lying on his bed, his guitar slung across his body. "Everyone heads for this place," he sang darkly, staring up at the ceiling. "The final home."

Euri floated in the middle of the room, watching him. At first, her expression was gentle. But then the song ended and an angry look returned to her face. She stuck her hand in the pocket of her blazer and pulled out a cockroach, throwing it onto the man's bed. He kicked at it with his foot and dropped his guitar. "Leave me alone!" he cried out. "Please."

Jack flew through the window and into the cluttered room. "It was him."

Euri started and turned around.

"At Grand Central," Jack continued. "When you jumped."

Euri began to pick at her skirt. "Well, you're a real Sherlock Holmes, aren't you?"

"Why didn't he stop you?"

"I don't want to talk about it."

There was a hard edge to Euri's voice that warned Jack

not to ask again. The musician settled back down with his guitar.

"What's his name?" Jack asked after a moment.

"Nate," Euri whispered.

"Did he always play guitar?"

Euri nodded.

"How did you meet?"

"One day after school. In the park. He knew one of my friends. He played this song for me. . . ." Euri smiled at the memory.

A rapping sound on the window made them both turn around. It was Cora. Euri's smile vanished. Jack stood up and opened the window to let Cora in.

"I want to get a message to my mom," she said.

Euri shot her an annoyed stare. "Which part of being in the underworld do you not understand? The living-people-not-hearing-you part or the living-people-not-hearing-you part?"

Cora held up the *Unofficial Guide*. "It says here that we can talk to the living with a Ouija board. Maybe we can get someone living to pass along a message to my mom?"

"Wait a second," said Jack. "That's it!"

"What's it?" said Euri.

"Dr. Lyons," Jack explained. "He can help us find Viele!"

"Who's Dr. Lyons?" asked Cora.

"He's a doctor of the paranormal," Jack explained. "Last time I was here we talked to him through his Ouija board. We can have him contact your mom and also look for more information about Viele."

"That's the best idea you've had so far," Euri said.

Cora eagerly held out her hand. "Let's go."

Jack was relieved that they had a plan, but he noticed that Cora still wouldn't look him in the eye. As they flew over the crowded streets of the Lower East Side, Euri taking the lead, he reminded himself that they still had two nights. If Dr. Lyons helped them find Viele, there was a chance he could get Cora home. Perhaps his dream had been a good omen.

And that was when he saw him. Austin—Jack was certain of it—was standing on the sidewalk outside St. Mark's Comics, talking to a familiar-looking plump ghost. Before Jack could do anything, the ghost offered Austin his hand, and they flew off together toward downtown.

XVIII | The Sting

Jack stopped flying and hovered in the air. "I saw him."

"Saw who?" said Cora absently.

"Austin."

"I knew that was him before!" Cora scanned the sidewalk below. "Where?"

"He flew off," said Jack. "With another ghost. But he was right there." He pointed to the sidewalk outside the comic-book store.

Euri circled back. "What's the holdup?"

"I saw Austin."

At the mention of Austin's name, Euri gave him a cross look. "That's impossible."

"No, Cora's right. He's really in the underworld. Why didn't he go back?"

Cora's eyes narrowed as she began to chew on an imaginary piece of gum. "Maybe he didn't want to," she said slowly.

"What do you mean?" Jack asked.

"His brother. He's never mentioned him before. Maybe it's because he's dead? Maybe Austin figured out where we were when he saw Euri, and ran off to find him?"

Cora's theory made more sense than Jack wanted to admit. He had done the same thing on his last visit—stayed to search for his mom.

"That's ridiculous," said Euri. "You probably saw someone else. But you can't worry about him now, anyway. You need to worry about yourselves."

"Euri's right," said Jack. "We need to find Viele first. Then we can worry about Austin."

"I just know that's what happened," Cora said with a sigh.

As they flew toward Dr. Lyons's building, Jack tried not to think about Austin. Instead, he told Cora everything he knew about Dr. Lyons, though he omitted the story of his last visit and how Dr. Lyons had given him the recipe for the ghost-repellent pouch. "I hope he'll be able to help us," said Cora when he was done.

"I'm sure he will," said Jack as they shot up to the twenty-third floor, Euri racing ahead of them. "Is he there?" he called up to Euri as she landed on the ledge outside Dr. Lyons's window.

Euri stuck out her hand, palm-down, in a stop signal and then put her finger to her lips. Jack knew instantly something was wrong.

"What is . . . ?" Cora asked.

"Shhh," said Jack.

Quietly, they joined Euri on the ledge and peered through the window into the run-down, candlelit office. Dr. Lyons was sitting at his desk, one hand on his Ouija board, just as Jack had hoped he would be. But sitting across from him was a squat, muscular guard.

"Who are you?" Dr. Lyons asked out loud as he spelled out the sentence with his indicator.

"**Y-O-U-R L-O-N-G L-O-S-T F-A-T-H-E-R**," the guard spelled back.

"But my father is still alive," said Dr. Lyons.

"Damn," said the guard.

Another guard with a face that reminded Jack of a bull-dog's leafed through Dr. Lyons's books. "You're not supposed to be doing that," he said. "If Inspector Kennedy . . ."

"Why didn't we get to patrol one of the streams?" the squat guard interrupted. "Catch the Living Avenger trying to escape—end up in the paper."

But just as the words were out of his mouth, a third, wiry guard blew through the door. "Someone's coming!"

All three guards vanished, one down through the floor and two up through the ceiling. A woman in a bell-shaped dress and carrying a parasol floated through the door next to a man with a bowler hat and mustache. Jack recognized the ghosts from his last visit to Dr. Lyons's office. He wished there was a way he could warn them about the guards, but every few moments, he noticed the top of a guard's head, peeking up through the floor or down through the ceiling, then darting back.

"Are you sure we should have come back?" the man asked in a tense whisper. "After what happened last time . . ."

"I'm still not certain that was the Living Avenger," the woman stated definitively. "That thing could have been a ghost who had just died, so it looked alive."

Jack scowled, annoyed at being called a "thing."

The man in the bowler hat gave his companion a skeptical look. "I know what I saw," he said firmly.

"Anyway, Dr. Lyons has no living patients," the woman continued. She floated over to Dr. Lyons and kissed him on one of his round cheeks. "Hello, Doctor."

"My long-dead grandfather, maybe?" Dr. Lyons said, unaware of the greeting.

The woman, with a sweep of her skirts, floated opposite Dr. Lyons and put her hands on the Ouija board indicator as the man peered nervously around the office. "Y-O-U-R F-R-I-E-N-D-S F-R-O-M T-H-E O-T-H-E-R S-I-D-E . . ." the woman began to spell.

But before she could finish, the guards shot up out of the floor and down through the ceiling. The candles flickered. "Freeze!" they shouted.

"Clarabelle!" the man yelped.

But it was too late. The guards grabbed both ghosts as the Ouija board indicator toppled to the floor.

"Did I do that?" Dr. Lyons asked, picking up the indicator.

"You have been apprehended performing an illegal underworld activity," the squat guard read to the two ghosts from a small book. "Anything you say can and will be held against you."

"Surely this is a misdemeanor offense?" asked the now trembling ghost in the bowler hat.

A loud bark startled him as Cerberus bounded through the door followed by a hefty ghost with piercing blue eyes. The guards saluted him.

"At ease," he said.

One of Cerberus's heads, catching sight of Jack and Cora through the window, began to bark and whine. "Heel!" the hefty ghost shouted.

"Time to go," Euri whispered.

"I want to see what happens," said Jack.

"And maybe they'll all leave soon," whispered Cora. "And we can Ouija with Dr. Lyons."

"Commissioner Kennedy," said the squat guard to the ghost with piercing blue eyes. "We've apprehended two suspects. Caught 'em in the act."

"Please, Commissioner," begged the ghost in the

bowler hat. "It was our first time. We didn't mean any harm!"

Kennedy looked unmoved. "That's for the courts to decide."

Suddenly, one of Cerberus's heads let out a spine-tingling howl, and the beast began trying to charge over to the window.

Jack tensed, preparing to dive off the ledge with Cora.

"I told you we should go," Euri whispered.

"Stop it," Kennedy shouted at Cerberus. "We've caught them already!"

The man blanched. "The courts?"

"There's a Security Alert going on," Kennedy explained sternly. "'The law hath not been dead, though it hath slept.'"

The squat guard scrunched up his face. "Who said that, boss?"

Kennedy peered down at him with disdain. "Shakespeare."

The woman in the bell-shaped dress began to weep. "Have mercy! I've had such a hard death!"

Dr. Lyons put the indicator back on the Ouija board and placed his fingers on it. "Anyone there?" he asked.

Kennedy sneered at him and then glowered at the sobbing ghost. "Tell it to the judge." He turned to the guards. "Good work, boys. I'll call for reinforcements to take these two down to the courthouse. Continue your undercover work here."

Jack watched as Kennedy saluted and pulled Cerberus out the door.

"They're not leaving," said Cora, peering at the guards with obvious disappointment. "What are we going to do now?"

Dr. Lyons sighed and stood up. "Slow night," he murmured to himself, putting on a raincoat.

Jack looked at the two ghosts. Tears were still streaming down the woman's face, and the guards had taken away her parasol. The man in the bowler hat floated quietly above Dr. Lyons's ratty couch, unable to look at her. Jack wished he could have warned them. "I hope they at least get a good lawyer," he whispered to Euri.

"I wouldn't worry," said Euri. "There are lawyers who have worked at the courthouse for centuries."

"Centuries?" said Jack with a sly grin.

"What is it?" said Cora.

"Eleanor Fletcher Bishop said Viele was always suing people. If there are lawyers who've worked there for centuries, someone must know him. Maybe they can help us track down where he is!"

Cora turned to Euri. "Can you take us to the courthouse?"

"Sure, but night court for the living doesn't close until

one A.M., and night court for the dead only opens after that."

"One A.M.!" said Cora. "Half the night will be over." She turned to Jack. "I want to check on my mom."

"No," said Euri before Jack could answer.

"You haunt that guy in the tenement every night," Cora snapped. "Why can't I haunt my mom?"

"Because you're not dead," said Euri.

"Yet," said Cora glumly.

"Euri's right," Jack added softly. "It's probably better for us to—" But he didn't know what it would be better for them to do. Besides the courthouse, he was completely out of leads.

"—do something fun," Euri finished.

Jack and Cora looked at her in surprise.

She shrugged. "It's not every night you get to do whatever you want in Manhattan." She looked at Cora. "Especially you. I bet you can't do anything because of your mom."

"That's not true," Cora said halfheartedly.

"You do usually go home pretty early," said Jack.

"Jack's plan is a good one," said Euri. "But you can't just dwell on your mom while you wait for the court to open." Before Cora could protest, Euri grabbed her free hand and pulled them both away from Dr. Lyons's window.

The first place Euri took them wasn't one Jack would have chosen himself: Saks Fifth Avenue, the enormous department store with fancy window displays of mannequins in designer clothes. The store was closed, but as they floated up the escalator, they passed perfectly coiffed ghosts gaping over the new offerings in the shoe department and whippet-thin spirits in sunglasses critiquing the fall line of couture clothing. "Can we try stuff on?" asked Cora.

"The dead can't change their clothes, so they just window shop," Euri explained, casting a doleful glance at her uniform. "But you two can."

"I'll just watch," said Jack as they floated onto a floor filled with airy racks of ball gowns.

Euri ordered Cora into an empty dressing room while she flew around picking dresses for her to try on. A minute later, she returned with a canary yellow, diamond-encrusted gown and what looked to Jack like a purple tutu with half a dead leopard attached to the top, and a leather jacket and blue silk shirt, which she held out to Jack.

"These are for you. You definitely need a makeover."

"No," he protested. "I'm not trying that on."

"Come on, Jack," Cora yelled from the dressing room. "I'm doing it!"

"You heard her," Euri snickered.

With a sigh, Jack retreated to the dressing room. When he emerged, Cora was sashaying around the racks in the canary yellow gown as Euri pretended to take photos of her. As much as Euri had meant to hate Cora, Jack realized that she had made a friend. He cleared his throat, and they both turned around and began to clap.

"What an improvement," said Euri. She turned to Cora. "Now if we could just do something about his hair."

Cora laughed and Jack felt himself blush. "Can we go now?"

A half hour later, after they had forced him into snakeskin pants, a velvet smoking jacket, and a ruffled white shirt that reminded Jack of something a pirate might wear, he finally convinced them that it was time to go somewhere else. They flew downtown to a nightclub called Webster Hall, where Euri flirted with a burly ghost bouncer and finally convinced him that Cora had been dead long enough to be admitted. They joined the throngs of the living and dead, dancing to techno beats and strobe lights on the club's six differently themed dance floors. Then, with their eardrums still pulsing, they flew to the Strand bookstore near Union Square, where they roamed the eighteen miles of musty, used books, sharing with each other the strangest titles: Euri chose *Better to Never Have Been: The Harm of Coming into Existence*, while Cora offered *The Stray Shopping Carts of Eastern North America:*

A Guide to Field Identification. The entire time, Jack secretly kept an eye out for Austin but never spotted him. Finally, just before one, he glanced at his watch and nudged Euri. It was time to go to court.

XIX | Mann Down

At a quarter to one, they floated down in front of a tall, dingy building with narrow windows on the edge of Chinatown.

"One Hundred Centre Street," Euri said, gesturing toward it. Although the municipal buildings around it looked dark and closed, several stories of 100 Centre Street were illuminated by fluorescent lights, and police cruisers and New York City Corrections vans idled in front of it. A few worn-out-looking living people stood in the blazing lights just outside the entrance, smoking cigarettes or talking furtively on their cell phones. A trio of ghosts huddled together whispering to each other, in front of the words WHERE THE LAW ENDS TYRANNY BEGINS engraved on the wall. One of them looked up and shot a suspicious glance at Cora.

"Try not to look anyone in the eye," Euri reminded her as they floated toward the bronze-and-glass doors with the words SOUTH ENTRANCE embossed above them.

Cora nodded. Since leaving the Strand, Jack noticed that she had grown pensive again.

They floated through the glass door and into a brightly lit lobby where a pair of uniformed living guards sat in front of a metal detector. Across from them floated a dead guard who pointed to a sign affixed to the front of it. IT IS A SERIOUS VIOLATION OF THE LAW TO BRING A OUIJA BOARD INTO A MUNICIPAL COURTHOUSE.

"We're clean," said Euri.

The dead guard held out a plastic container. "Any charms, chains, channeling devices?" she droned.

Cora, carefully looking down at the ground, shook her head. Jack suddenly remembered the ghost repellent. It would probably count as a charm. He was relieved he had given it to Austin.

"We're looking for ghosts who might have worked in the court system in the 1800s," said Euri.

"Try Room 130," said the guard, pointing down a marble hallway.

They floated down the hallway, past banks of pay phones and into a crowded corridor. A line of living people snaked out of a door that read ARRAIGNMENT INFORMATION, while others huddled on wooden benches. They flew past them through a set of heavy wooden doors and into a large, fluorescently lit courtroom with high ceilings and recessed windows covered with maroon drapes. Jack immediately scanned the room for ghosts in nineteenth-century dress, but while it bustled with activity, it was entirely of the living variety. Defendants slumped on wooden benches in one corner of the courtroom while public defenders in cheap suits scurried around the courtroom conferring with prosecutors and police. Officers of the court milled about, handcuffs jiggling on their hips as they shushed the family members and other onlookers who sat in a gallery at the back of the room. In the front, a black-robed, double-chinned judge perched on a dais, yawning as a prosecutor read charges against three men who stood in front of him. "Where are the dead?" Jack whispered to Euri.

"It's not one o'clock yet," she said, floating over to one of the benches in the gallery and taking a seat.

"Don't worry," said Jack as he led Cora over to the bench. "I'm sure some ghosts will be here soon. One of them will know Viele."

Because of the high ceilings, it was hard to hear what anyone was saying, but Jack finally made out that the three men were accused of stealing 213 pairs of sneakers. The judge released them to their families, set a court date, and then pounded his gavel. "This session of New York City criminal court has adjourned for the night," he said. He stood up and waddled out a door Jack hadn't noticed before at the back of the courtroom. The public defenders and prosecutors gathered up their folders and left the courtroom. The onlookers filed out of the gallery.

"Is that it?" Cora asked, looking around at the empty courtroom.

Suddenly, one of the maroon drapes rustled and a court officer emerged. A rush of onlookers flew through the double doors into the gallery, some in long dresses, wailing and clutching handkerchiefs, others wearing fedora hats and carrying notebooks, one lugging an enormous camera with a round flash as large as his head. Several cops in double-breasted jackets and helmets floated through a door behind the defendant's bench, escorting half-a-dozen ghosts, some of whom covered their faces, others who looked defiantly out at the crowd. Then a noisy group of attorneys dropped down through the ceiling.

"All rise for The Honorable Judge Joseph M. Deuel," announced the bailiff as a stout, robed man with a big, white handlebar mustache blew through the door at the back of the courtroom. Everyone respectfully floated a few feet higher as the judge took his seat. "Case 1023453," read the bailiff. "*The People versus Mortimer Stewart and Clarabelle Stewart.*"

The ghost with the bowler hat was led from the defendant's bench to the desk in front of the judge followed by the woman with the bell-shaped skirt.

Accompanying them was a jaunty ghost with tufts of red hair sticking up from his head.

"Hey, look!" said Cora. "Those were the ghosts in Dr. Lyons's office."

"On October fifth," a gray-haired prosecutor somberly intoned, "Mortimer Stewart and Clarabelle Stewart flew into a well-documented hot spot of illegal paranormal activity and attempted to make contact with the living using a Ouija board. We have witnesses to the crime, two underworld security officers who have filed sworn affidavits—Exhibit A."

"It was our first time," Clarabelle Stewart interrupted, her face turning red.

Her attorney whispered something into her ear and then turned to the judge. "Your Honor," he said with a flourish of his hand, "my client has never violated any underworld laws. She is working assiduously toward moving on and is not a danger to underworld society."

"Your Honor," said the prosecutor. "Let me remind you that we are under a Security Alert. These are dangerous times. The Living Avenger may have accomplices just like Mr. and Mrs. Stew—"

A murmur rose up from the gallery. "Silence in the court!" shouted the judge.

"Objection!" interrupted the Stewarts' red-haired attorney. "Your Honor, I ask that that be stricken from the record. There's no evidence that my clients have had any association with the Living Avenger."

"Absolutely!" Jack couldn't help shouting out.

"Motion granted," said Judge Deuel, stroking his mustache. "But I still find this charge quite serious. Sir and madam, you will remain in custody indefinitely." The judge struck his gavel.

"That didn't seem fair at all," whispered Cora.

"I wish I could have warned them," said Jack.

"It's too late now," Euri said. "So which lawyer do you think looks like he could have practiced when Viele was alive?"

Before the once-again weeping Clarabelle Stewart and her grim-looking husband could leave the stand, the ghost with the enormous camera leaned over the rope separating the gallery from the court and took their photo several times, the flash bursting across the room. As Jack watched him, he suddenly noticed an elderly ghost with a sweeping white beard dressed in a long waistcoat and a wide-brimmed hat. He stood beside the photographer, tipping a wooden walking stick at the judge who smiled and nodded back at him. Jack elbowed his friends. "How about that guy?"

Cora leaned forward. "He seems to be dressed like someone from the nineteenth century."

The elderly man turned around and stared back at

them. Then he tapped the photographer's shoulder and whispered something in his ear.

"Let's go over and talk to him," said Jack.

"Hold on," said Euri, pointing to three furtive-looking ghosts floating up to the stand. "There's another good case up."

"Forget it. I need to get back to my mom," said Cora. But just as she stood up, the photographer swung around and took a photo of all three of them. Then he flew out of the courtroom.

Euri jumped out of her seat and pulled Cora back down. "Great! Now he's got a photo of us."

Cora shrugged. "So?"

The elderly man floated into the row of benches in front of them. "Hello," he said, turning to Cora with a smile.

"Hello," she asked eagerly. "We were just wondering. Did you work here in the nineteenth century?"

The man chuckled. "In a fashion."

Jack had an uncomfortable feeling.

"You wouldn't happen to remember an Egbert Viele?"

"General Viele, the water engineer?" said the ghost pleasantly. "But of course. Viele was from an illustrious New York family—his mother, as you may know, was a Knickerbocker. I am from a similarly important background—the Manns of Sandusky, Ohio." He studied their blank faces. "I guess you haven't heard of them. But we both served our glorious Union during the war. Now, why would you be looking for him?"

Cora turned to Jack. But before he could help her come up with a reason, the old ghost grinned, revealing his teeth, and leaned close to Cora. "Let me guess," he said. "Perhaps because you're alive? And you're looking for a way out of the underworld?"

"She's not alive," Euri insisted, shifting her eyes.

The old man raised his cane and waved over the photographer who had reappeared flapping a Polaroid. "This is Weegee, the celebrated crime photographer. And I am Colonel William D'Alton Mann, former editor of *Town Topics*, the most famous weekly magazine chronicling New York City manners and high society. I now write Mann Down, the preeminent column in *The Underworld Times*. I have many readers, including the guards, who enjoy my column a great deal. We share tips, you know."

Jack exchanged an alarmed glance with Cora.

Weegee pointed to the photo in his hand. "You're right, Colonel, she's alive."

"As you can see," Colonel Mann continued, taking the photo and showing it to Euri, Cora, and Jack, "we have proof." He nodded at Weegee. "Good work, sir. Carry on."

As Weegee flew away to snap pictures of the next set of defendants, Jack studied his photo. Everyone in the courtroom was faded except for Cora. His own transparent face looked as dead as the rest of the ghosts. Cora noticed this and shot him a puzzled look.

"My column prints only veracities," Colonel Mann continued, "and sometimes photos. This one of the Living Avenger will be the talk of the town—especially down at the commissioner's office."

Jack shook his head, confused. "The Living Avenger?"

Colonel Mann twirled his cane. "So, to wit, a preview of tonight's column." He began to speak in a deep, theatrical voice. "'Mann Down Exclusive!! Is the Living Avenger a fan of our legal system? Why else did she show up in night court earlier this evening?'"

"*She?*" Jack repeated.

"That silly spirit in Central Park had the impression you were a boy," Mann said to Cora with an amused snort.

Jack considered revealing the truth. But having seen the photo, Colonel Mann was unlikely to believe that Jack could be the Living Avenger. He looked too dead to be the living anything.

"Hey, wait a minute!" said Euri.

But Colonel Mann ignored her. "Or maybe," he continued, with a flourish of his cane, "'What mysterious menace showed up at night court accompanied by two rather plain and annoying ghosts?'"

Euri looked seconds away from grabbing Colonel Mann's cane and whacking him over the head with it.

"Of course," the colonel added in a quiet voice, "should you be able to offer your assistance to the Mann Down column, I might be able to see to it that the story is not published tonight and the photo is returned."

"So is that how you work?" Euri muttered.

Cora's face was as red as Clarabelle Stewart's. "That's blackmail! I'm going to go tell the judge."

Before she could walk away, Euri grabbed on to the back of her shirt. "Don't be an idiot. He'll turn you over to the guards."

Colonel Mann yawned. "Or just back to me. Joe and I go way back. He was the lawyer for *Town Topics*."

Euri crossed her arms over her chest. "So what do you want from us?"

"It's rather simple," said the Colonel. "There's a woman who did me a bad turn when we were alive. She teaches a class now every night at two A.M. at the Colony Club. I want the Living Avenger to show up there and cause a scene. I'll send Weegee to take some photos. But I promise not to print any that include the Living Avenger."

Euri narrowed her eyes. "Why should we trust you?"

Colonel Mann chuckled. "Because if you don't, I'll just print this photo of the Living Avenger at night court in tonight's edition of my column." He pointed at Cora.

"The paper comes out at four A.M. The guards will have you locked up in seconds flat."

"Plus," he continued pleasantly. "I do know more about Mr. Viele—and you're right to be looking for him if you want to get this young lady back. Meet me at Delmonico's when you're done and I'll return this photo and tell you more."

XX | How to Treat an Underworld Guest

"Forget it," said Euri, as soon as they'd flown out of the courthouse. "We still have time before the paper comes out and the guards go after Cora. Let's just keep looking for Viele on our own."

Jack looked at Dylan Thomas's pocket watch and shook his head. "Less than three hours."

"So you're saying you trust Mann?" asked Euri.

"I'm not sure," Jack admitted. "But he could have just turned Cora in right there. Think of the headline: 'Mann Down Exclusive! Mann Down Nabs Living Avenger in Crowded Courtroom.' Instead he wants to get back at this person who hurt him during his life. That seems real to me."

They both turned to Cora. She hadn't said a word since they'd left the courthouse, chewing on another invisible piece of gum.

"What do you think?" Jack asked her.

"We don't have any other leads about Viele," she said finally. "I think we need to do what Mann says."

Reluctantly, Euri led them uptown. As they sailed over the little parks near the courthouse, Foley Square, and Collect Pond Park, Cora turned to Jack. "Why didn't you show up in that photo?" she asked.

Jack told her about the photos Dr. Lyons took of him—how he, but nothing else in the room, had come out overexposed.

"So you're sort of like a ghost yourself?"

"But I'm alive," Jack insisted, thinking of the guard who was certain he looked dead at the library. "I just have some paranormal abilities."

"Is that why they call you the Living Avenger?"

Jack nodded. "Even when I'm in the living world, I can see ghosts. Sometimes they realize I can see them and get frightened." He told her about the ghost he had shouted at in Central Park (though he didn't tell her the exact reason why) and the Mann Down column about how the Living Avenger had terrorized a ghost in Central Park.

"So if I'm supposed to act like the Living Avenger now," Cora asked, "what should I do?"

"Create a scene," said Euri. "Shout at people. Act crazy. It'll be fun."

Jack could tell Euri wished she could be the Living Avenger.

As they turned onto Park Avenue, Cora practiced fierce expressions, grimacing and scowling and raising a threatening fist. Jack looked away so he wouldn't laugh.

"Think of things that make you angry," coached Euri.

"Like being stuck in the underworld?"

"Exactly. And not being thin."

Cora's face turned red and her eyebrows furrowed. She glared at Euri.

"That's better," said Euri. "And all the people who've done you wrong."

"Like who?" Cora asked, still looking annoyed by the fat comment. "You?"

"Well, there's Jack."

"Thanks," Jack interrupted. "I think she's probably ready to go now."

They floated up Park Avenue to a regal four-story red brick and marble building on the northwest corner of Sixty-second Street. Euri led them under a blue awning and toward a heavy wood door with a stained glass arch above it.

"What's this place called again?" asked Jack.

"The Colony Club," said Euri as they flew into a rotunda-shaped, cream-colored lobby decorated with tall, dark vases and a giant cast-iron chandelier. "It's the city's oldest private club for women."

"Clearly not just *any* women," said Cora, pointing to a series of large oil portraits of stern-looking women in triple-strands of pearls and feathered hats.

"No, wealthy women, social-register types," said Euri.

As Euri peered around the lobby, looking for signs announcing the class, a trio of ghosts carrying squash rackets made an unnecessarily wide arc around them, and an elderly woman in an outdated swimsuit that looked like a dress floated up through the floor and asked Jack to fetch her a drink. But before he could explain to her that he was not, in fact, a waiter, a tall ghost in a sweeping black dress and large feathered hat emerged from the corner of the lobby and cleared her throat. Jack recognized her from one of the portraits.

"Can I help you?" she said in an unhelpful voice.

"We're here for the class," said Euri.

The ghost looked the three of them up and down. "You were invited?"

Euri crossed her arms as if to challenge her. "Of course."

"Even"—the ghost made a dismissive gesture at Jack with one hand—"him?"

"He was especially requested," Euri said.

The ghost wrinkled her nose. "Very well," she said, "they're up in the library."

They followed her through the ceiling into a library with floral-patterned armchairs and row upon row of dark wood bookshelves. A circle of women in long white nightgowns, boat-necked silk dresses, and velvet ball gowns floated in the center of the room. A tall, gray-haired ghost with a small black hat perched at an odd angle on her head and large pearl earrings floated at the circle's head and beckoned them to join.

"Just because one is dead does not mean that one should be rude," she instructed. "For example, there has been a tragic decline in what I shall call 'flying manners.' It has become commonplace for ghosts to carelessly whip around the corners of buildings, nearly crashing into others."

A few of the ghosts nodded in recognition.

"One should slow down before turning and proffer a salutation to others traveling past, such as 'Good Evening,' or if the traveler is an acquaintance, a friendly inquiry such as, 'How is your Aunt Millie? Has she moved on?'"

The ghosts murmured in assent.

Jack suddenly noticed Weegee perched on the windowsill outside the library. He waved to Jack and then lifted a finger to his lips.

"New York, more than any city in the world, honors authenticity, wit, and originality, and so will allow for variation in manners," the gray-haired woman continued. "But I am appalled by the behavior of many poltergeists. Screaming, interfering with lights or plumbing, or otherwise drawing attention toward oneself in an untoward manner are not the hallmarks of a well-bred spirit."

Jack noticed Euri begin to pick at her skirt.

"Weegee's here," Jack whispered.

"Good," said Euri, looking up with relief. "Cora, you're on."

Cora took a deep breath and stood up. "I am the Living Avenger!" she shouted.

A communal gasp rose up from the lady ghosts. Someone shrieked. Jack noticed Weegee raise his camera.

"Stop!" declared the gray-haired ghost with the small black hat. "Stop it all of you!" Floating over to Cora, the gray-haired woman seized her hand and shook it firmly. "How do you do, Miss Avenger? I am Emily Post, the etiquette expert, and I am honored to have you at my manners class."

Cora shook her hand and then confused, pulled it away. "I'm the Living Avenger," she said weakly.

"Yes and I'm Mrs. Post. Emily, if you will." Mrs. Post gently scolded the other ghosts. "The hallmark of a polite spirit is treating every guest to the underworld with equal respect—whether they are dead or alive."

Euri shot out of her seat. "No, you have to act terrified!"

Mrs. Post raised a single eyebrow. "I beg your pardon?"

"The Living Avenger is terrorizing the city! Now she's come to terrorize your class!"

Mrs. Post gave Cora a sympathetic look. "You don't seem very terrorizing."

Jack noticed Weegee put down his camera, perplexed. What if he flew away and told Colonel Mann that they had betrayed him?

"Wait!" said Jack. "I have an etiquette question."

Mrs. Post turned to him.

"Say you've been blackmailed by a newspaper columnist who's threatened to publish photos that will jeopardize the life of someone"—Jack felt himself blush—"very special. The only way to stop him is to get one of his enemies to act terrorized so the columnist can publish photos of her instead."

Mrs. Post frowned. "So my old friend Colonel Mann is behind this. After he tried to blackmail my husband, Edwin, I encouraged Edwin to involve the police. The Colonel ended up in a very compromising court trial about the real nature of his gossip column. The right thing to do is to resist his demands."

Jack noticed Weegee glance impatiently behind him into the night. He clearly couldn't hear their conversation and was losing interest. "But we need to find Egbert Viele," Jack begged. "And Colonel Mann has promised to help."

"Viele, the engineer?" piped up a tiny, shriveled ghost in an ostrich-feather hat.

"That's right," said Jack, hoping she would know something. He pulled out Viele's maps and reports and floated over to show her. "He made these."

She flipped through the reports and maps, stopping at the one of Central Park. "I forgot what a wasteland it was before they built the park," she remarked.

Cora pointed to the scattering of squares. "But what are these?"

"Squatters," the ghost replied dismissively. "Mostly free blacks, a few illiterate Germans and Irish. The city evicted them when it built the park. Made it a much nicer place."

"Do you know where to find Viele?" Cora asked.

The ghost regretfully shook her head. "I'm afraid not."

"We can't help you," added Mrs. Post gently.

Jack floated over to Cora, who was deep in thought, chewing her phantom piece of gum. "We better go," he said glumly.

"Wait," Cora said. She turned to Mrs. Post. "If you're so into manners, isn't the proper thing to do to put your guests' comfort and well-being before your own?"

The lady ghosts murmured in assent.

"Of course it is," said Mrs. Post. "But in a case of blackmail—"

"Your guests will need to depend on your hospitality even more," Cora interrupted. "Won't you please, just for a minute, act frightened of me?"

For a moment, Mrs. Post looked uncertainly at Cora. Then, with a loud shriek, she pulled at her hair and nearly crashed into the wall. "The Living Avenger!!!" she cried.

"She's come for us!" shouted the ghost in the ostrich-feather hat, pretending to faint as she slumped against an armchair.

Suddenly all the lady ghosts started flying in distressed circles, clutching their hands together, wailing and pointing at Cora who, with a look of delight, began to chase them around the library. Euri took the opportunity to fly from armchair to armchair, jumping and shouting.

Weegee, Jack noticed, had stuck his head through the window and was hurriedly taking photo after photo. After a few minutes, he gave Jack a thumbs-up and flew back through the window into the night.

XXI | Delmonico's

"These are good, quite good," said Colonel Mann, a note of surprise in his voice as his thick fingers flipped through the stack of photos that Weegee had dropped off just moments earlier.

They were sitting at a table in the back of Delmonico's restaurant on Beaver Street, which was a winding lane lined with small stores and barbershops. The restaurant was closed for the night, but inside its heavy wood-paneled rooms, ghosts in enormous hats, silk dresses, and tuxedos hovered above the dark brown leather chairs, looking very much like the mural of elegantly dressed people dining at Delmonico's on the walls. Waiters in blue shirts and tan vests with the Delmonico's emblem flew through the dining rooms, carrying trays of drinks and greeting patrons by name. "I've been coming here since 1837," Jack overheard one ghost tell another, "and the service has never been better!"

Colonel Mann held up a photo of Emily Post in

mid-screech and laughed heartily, tapping the ground appreciatively with his walking stick. "Charles!" he shouted.

A dapper ghost rushed up to the table, notebook in hand.

"Take dictation." Colonel Mann cleared his throat. "'Mann Down Exclusive. Exclamation point. Make that three exclamation points. Mann Down has learned that moronic manners maven Emily Post got the fright of her death when the Living Avenger paid a visit to her etiquette class at the Colony Club earlier this evening. "That silly socialite was scared stiff," confided one witness.'"

"That sounds like you," said Jack to the colonel.

The colonel winked at Jack. "'Luckily our fearless photographer caught some of the action.' Charles, let's make that tonight's lead item!"

Charles nodded. "Very well, sir. I'll take it directly to the newsroom."

"We fulfilled our end of the deal," said Euri curtly once Charles had left. "Now it's time for you to fulfill yours."

"You're supposed to tell us about General Viele," said Jack.

"And give us back the courtroom photo," added Euri.

Colonel Mann slipped the Polaroid out of his breast pocket. "Here you go," he said, sliding it across the table.

Euri snatched it up, looked it over, then handed it to Jack.

Mann laughed. "Don't worry, I've kept my promise."

"Half of it," said Euri.

"Drinks?"

Euri scowled. "You know they can't have them."

Colonel Mann's eyes narrowed. "What do you mean, *they*?"

Euri blinked. "I mean Cora, because she's alive. And Jack—"

"Because I'm underage," Jack interrupted. "I'm fifteen and I just died a few weeks ago."

"Could have fooled me," Colonel Mann said. "You look more dead than that. But it hardly matters. The waiters will serve any friend of Colonel Mann's, no questions asked."

"That's okay," said Jack, troubled that once again he looked so dead.

"We don't want drinks," Euri said. "We want Viele. Where is he?"

Colonel Mann opened his eyes wide in a feigned show of surprise. "My dear girl, I never said I knew where he was. I only said I could tell you more about him."

"You don't know where he is?" asked Cora.

"But you're right to look for him!" Colonel Mann thundered. He leaned across the table and lowered his voice. "My sources tell me his map was used for an escape attempt just last year."

"Now, there's a news flash," said Euri.

"Viele knows other ways out, too," Mann continued in a whisper. "Ways not on the map. Ways even the guards don't know. That's why they keep his haunt classified. They don't want him found."

Jack squeezed Cora's hand under the table. "We know he made some other maps. One of Central Park—"

"Do you think he might haunt it?" Cora asked.

Colonel Mann snorted. "Viele haunt Central Park?"

Jack came to Cora's defense. "Well, he must have helped build it, right?"

The Colonel shouted out to a couple of ghosts floating at the table next to him. "Who designed Central Park?"

"Frederick Law Olmsted and Calvert Vaux," roared back a man in a waistcoat.

"Right," said Colonel Mann. Then he added in a loud whisper, "But not if you believe General Viele."

"What do you mean?" asked Cora.

"Viele was originally appointed chief engineer for the park and had his own plan for how to design it. But in the competition for who would design the park, his plan lost out to Olmsted and Vaux's. So being the belligerent man he was, he—"

"Sued them," Jack said, thinking of what Eleanor Fletcher Bishop had said about Viele always being in court.

Colonel Mann nodded. "Exactly. He claimed they had copied his design."

"Did he win?" asked Cora.

Colonel Mann shrugged. "Some back pay for his surveying efforts. But in the court of public opinion, he lost. His plan had some similarities to Olmsted and Vaux's but theirs was the better one. Throughout his life he referred to himself as the park's creator, but no one thought of him as having had anything to do with it. He was very bitter about it."

Jack suddenly felt sorry for Viele. "But he did do all this other stuff with water."

"No one thinks about water," said Mann. "But everyone loves Central Park."

"What else can you tell us about him?" Euri asked.

Colonel Mann gave an amused smile. "You flatter my intelligence. All I know is that Viele is this young lady's ticket home." He turned to Cora and held out something small and brown. "Bonbon, my dear?"

"Sure," said Cora. But just as she reached out her palm, Jack knocked the chocolate out of Colonel Mann's hand. He could feel his heart pounding in his chest.

"You can't eat!" he said.

"I know," Cora whispered. "I was just trying to be polite."

"But he wasn't," said Euri loudly, pointing to the colonel. She leaned across the table and hissed in his ear. "Why are you trying to kill her?"

Colonel Mann waved one protesting hand in the air. "I thought perhaps there could be a little glory for the Mann Down column. 'Fearless Columnist Single-Handedly Apprehends Living Avenger!'" he whispered. "She's going to die here anyway."

"No I'm not!" shouted Cora, jumping out of her seat.

Ghostly diners turned to stare.

"Weegee!" Mann shouted. "Photo op!"

"Let's get her out of here," said Euri.

Before the photographer could appear, they disappeared through the wall.

XXII | A Beautiful View

"I knew we couldn't trust him," Euri said.

They were flying aimlessly above the crooked streets of the financial district. They passed the white marble columns and sculpted frieze of the New York Stock Exchange, where a few ghost traders in blue and red jackets dashed inside, then circled the towering brownstone spire of Trinity Church. In the church cemetery, a few ghosts floated among the tilted, faded tombstones, looking for their names. Jack could tell from the living homeless, carefully positioned over the subway grates or wrapped in cardboard and wedged against the doors of the financial firms, that it had grown even colder.

He sneaked a glance at Cora. He could tell from her furrowed brow that she was still thinking about what Colonel Mann had said. He floated down to the front steps of Trinity Church and faced her. "You're not going to die," he said.

Cora looked away from him. "Don't keep saying that to me."

"But you're not. I promise—"

"My mom is always promising me she's not going to die," Cora interrupted.

Euri silently joined them.

"We all die," said Jack gently. "But I'm sure she won't for a long, long—"

"She's getting worse," Cora said, her voice cracking. "And now, I'm dying too."

"No, you're not!" Euri insisted. "We know Viele can get you out. And we know he hasn't moved on. We just need to figure out where he is."

"Austin!" said Cora.

Jack gave her a puzzled look. "What would he know?"

Cora pointed past Jack to something on the street. "No, look! There!"

His head down and his hands in his pocket, Austin was walking up Broadway. Beside him was the chubby ghost. Jack could clearly make out his features for the first time, and he suddenly realized why he looked so familiar—he had been in the tunnel with Dr. Earle when Jack had used the ghost repellent. The ghost must have found and befriended Austin after he ran off.

"Austin!" Cora shouted.

Austin turned around. But as soon as he caught sight

of them, he grabbed the ghost's hand and they hastily flew away.

"Hey, Austin," Jack shouted after him, "what are you doing? It's just us!"

They waited for him to turn around, but he never even looked back.

"Why is he avoiding us?" Cora asked as they watched him race uptown.

"Maybe he just wants to keep searching for his brother without us?" Jack offered. But secretly, he wondered if Austin was also mad at him. The chubby ghost must have explained to him that he was trapped, and now Austin wanted nothing to do with them.

"Maybe we should go after him?" said Cora. "Maybe if I talk to him?"

"Forget him for now," grumbled Euri. "We need to focus on finding Viele."

Cora gave her an exasperated look. "We're out of clues."

"Well, I guess there's no point, then," snapped Euri. "Maybe you should just go haunt your mom, and I should—"

"Why do you haunt the guy in the tenement, any-way?" Cora asked.

Euri's pale eyes shifted. "What does that have to do with anything?"

"Are you trying to move on?"

"No," Euri said tensely.

Cora's jaws began to work in the familiar gum-chewing motion. "But, wait, how exactly do you move on?"

"I told you I'm not moving on," Euri said.

"Not you. Ghosts in general."

Jack sensed that Cora was on to something. "You have to face up to the problems you had in life," he explained.

Cora chewed her imaginary gum thoughtfully. "Right. So when ghosts are getting ready to move on, they wouldn't haunt the places where they were successful. They'd haunt the people and places that made them unhappy, that made them feel like failures, so they could start facing up to them."

"I'm not trying to move on," Euri said.

"Not you," Cora repeated, her eyes flashing. "Viele! We know Viele wanted to design the park but failed. According to Colonel Mann, he was never able to face up to that failure. The guys in the tunnel said he's going to a place with a better view. Maybe he's trying to move on, maybe he's trying to come to terms with his failure."

"So where would he go?" asked Jack.

"The park," said Cora. "He'd have to go to the park!"

"Say you're right," Jack said. "That still leaves us with the problem of where in the park." He looked at his pocket watch. "We only have another hour or so till dawn."

"Where's Viele's Central Park map?" Cora asked.

Jack pulled it out of his backpack, and they all sat down on the stone steps to study it.

"Is there any place that looks like it could be a beautiful view?" Cora asked.

Euri shook his head. "There are a ton of places with beautiful views."

"Then we're just not seeing it," said Cora stubbornly.

Jack stared hard at the map. He scanned the hills and streams and squatters' camp and the reservoir in the center of the map that no longer existed. But there was nothing to see. *"Videre,"* he mumbled to himself.

Cora turned to him. "What did you just say?"

Jack felt his face turn red. *"Videre.* It just popped into my head. I just wish I could—"

" 'To see,' the root of the word 'view,' " Cora recited. She grabbed Jack's arm. *"Bellus!"*

Jack shook his head, not following. But then suddenly the two words came together and he leaped to his feet. *"Bellus videre.* That's it!"

XXIII | The Infiltration

"Belvedere Castle," Cora whispered. "Viele's got to be inside. It's too perfect."

They were floating just above a grassy knoll on the bank of Turtle Pond, looking out across the water at a miniature Victorian castle perched atop a jagged outcropping of rock. At this hour, Central Park was filled with ghosts. As they had flown across it, they had spotted them lining up at Bethesda Fountain, taking one last flight above the Ramble, hanging from the trees, as pale and translucent as the fluttering plastic bags occasionally tangled beside them in the branches. But Jack didn't see a single spirit floating around the castle. Only an American flag at the very top of the highest turret flapped in the wind. Jack pointed to it. "There must be a great view from up there."

"There's also probably a great view of who's coming," said Euri. "So how did you figure this out again?"

"*Bellus videre* is the Latin for a beautiful view," said Jack. "It's also the root of the word Belvedere." He scanned the balconies. "I don't see anyone standing watch."

"It doesn't matter. We know the guards don't want Viele to be found. We can't just fly in there and shout out his name." Euri held out her hands to them.

"What are you going to do?" Cora asked.

"We're going to have to sneak in," said Euri. "We don't have much time. Come on."

As soon as they took Euri's hands, she fell forward, pulling them down with her. But instead of hitting the ground, they hovered horizontally a few feet above it. Jack realized she was doing the aerial version of a stomach crawl. They skirted the banks of Turtle Pond, drifting just above the long grass toward the castle wall. At the wall, Euri turned them upright so they were pressed against the stone. Then they started to float up it, the rough-hewn schist blocks grazing Jack's nose. As soon as they reached a parapet, Euri poked her head above it and looked around. "All clear," she whispered.

They slid over the parapet and onto a balcony that overlooked the park. Jack could see the blinking lights of the city past the darkened clumps of trees. But before he could linger, Euri pulled him and Cora under a stone arch and into the castle. They drifted past an information desk, brochures and maps lined up across it, and into a darkened room filled with science exhibits and models of the park's wildlife. Euri led them in a quick circle around it, but there was no one—either dead or alive—inside. Just past the information desk, Jack noticed a set of narrow, winding stairs and silently pointed them out to Euri. She nodded and they began to float up them. As they spiraled around and around, Jack squeezed Cora's hand. He hoped they were right about the clue. If Viele wasn't at Belvedere castle, Jack had a feeling they would never find him.

"There's no one here," Cora whispered flatly as they reached the small landing at the top of the stairs.

Jack looked out through a narrow window. Just past Turtle Pond, he could see a dark clearing, illuminated at its edges by a few lights. "You can see the Great Lawn from here. But in Viele's time, that would have been the reservoir on his map. It would have been the perfect view for someone who cared about drinking water."

"It's a clever idea," Euri said gently. "But maybe Viele didn't know Latin."

Suddenly, from downstairs, Jack heard barking intermingled with loud voices.

"Take the mutt up to the tower!" a guard ordered. "See if there's someone there."

Jack tightened his grip on Cora's hand and looked up at the ceiling, planning their escape. And that's when he noticed the outline of a metal door in the ceiling. He grabbed Euri's arm and pointed. She nodded, and together, they flew up through it.

XXIV | The Mapmaker

They found themselves in a dimly lit circular room, barely larger than a closet. A balding gray-haired ghost dressed in a high-collared dark suit was floating by the one porthole-size window. He was small, not much taller than Cora, but had a big head and an oversized white walrus mustache. Jack was certain they had found Viele. But there was no time to confirm this. As heavy footsteps echoed up the stairwell below, Jack turned to the man and with a pleading expression, put his finger to his lips. Cerberus's thick body slammed against the walls as he clambered up the stairs, softly howling.

"Viele, is everything all right up there?" a deep voice shouted out.

Jack squeezed Cora's hand.

"Yes," said the mapmaker. "It's fine."

"We were just outside," the guard continued from the landing below. "The mutt thought he smelled someone alive near the pond, but we didn't find anyone. He's acting the same way now."

"There's no one here," Viele grumbled. "How am I supposed to move on if you keep disturbing me?"

Beneath them, they could hear the guard mutter, "Come on, you stupid beast," and a disappointed squeal from all three of Cerberus's heads as he was dragged back down the stairs.

As soon as the footsteps receded, Jack turned to Viele. "Thank you. I'm Jack. This is Cora and Euri."

Viele studied Jack's face with a look of curiosity. "Sorry about the dog. The guards want me to move on, you see. They don't want anyone to disturb me while I'm trying."

"Why?" asked Cora.

"Because I know more about the underworld than they do," Viele said. He pointed at Cora's eyes. "And because of living visitors who come searching for me like you. Each time I help them, I affect the living world, and it takes me longer to move on."

Euri grimaced. "Do you *want* to move on?"

The mapmaker shrugged. "Does anyone really want to? It's your problems that make you feel alive. Who wants to let go of the little hurts and pains that made you you?" He turned to Jack. "Though of course you don't realize that when you're living."

"So you think I'm alive?" asked Jack eagerly.

"I think you can be alive," Viele said, "if you choose."

Jack wanted to ask Viele what he meant but before he could, Euri cut in. "So if you don't want to move on, why are you here?" she asked, almost angrily.

"I never said I didn't want to," Viele corrected. "I just said it's hard." He frowned. "Do you know the story of Prospero?"

Jack nodded. "Shakespeare wrote a play about him. He's a sorcerer who lives on an island and controls everyone who lives there through magic."

"That's right," said Viele. "Do you know what he does at the end of the play?"

"He gets rid of his magic books."

Viele sighed. "I left my maps and papers behind. I stopped trying to order about the engineers in the water tunnel I used to haunt. I came back here to Central Park—the one place on this island where I never had any power—or at least the power I wanted to have. But it turns out that the hardest things to give up are the ones you never really controlled in the first place: how people feel about you, how the world remembers you—"

"But there are still things you can control," Euri interrupted. "Like helping Jack and Cora get back to the living world. There's a Security Alert. The guards are watching all the streams and rivers, including the one they came in through. But you must know another way out."

Viele closed his eyes, his expression pained. When he

opened them again, he gave a sad smile. "You're asking me to take up my wand again."

"If it were just me—" Jack began, but Euri flashed him a fierce look. "The thing is, Cora didn't choose to come here," he continued. "We need a second chance."

"I need to move on," Viele said quietly.

"Please," said Cora. "If I die, my mother . . ." She shook her head unable to go on.

The thump of boots followed by the clank of a chain leash as it dragged across stone suddenly echoed on the stairs below. "Viele!" A voice shouted. "They've just raised the Living Threat Level! We're coming up."

Jack quickly pulled Viele's maps and reports out of his backpack. "Just tell us where it is," he pleaded.

"I hear voices up there!" another guard shouted.

Viele yanked the map of Central Park out of the pile. "Here. You'll find epiphany in Seneca," he whispered as he handed it back to Jack.

Before Jack could ask Viele more, Cerberus, with a ferocious bark, leaped up through the trapdoor. Euri grabbed Cora's hand and yanked her into the air but not before one of Cerberus's heads pulled off her sneaker. The guard lunged at Jack, who flew up over his arms and out through the tower roof.

XXV | Seneca

They sped away from the castle, Euri leading the way with Cora. Jack, who had grabbed on to Cora's other hand, looked back over his shoulder. The sky was turning an inky blue and the silhouettes of trees and beyond them, tall apartment buildings, were gaining shape. But the guards continued to chase after them, Cerberus barking himself hoarse in the wind.

Below, a long line of ghosts waiting to dive into Bethesda Fountain snaked in winding circles around the stone terrace, moving steadily forward under the angel's impassive gaze. Euri swooped down to the fountain, slipping into the line. "Keep your heads down," she whispered. "Hopefully, we'll blend in with the crowd long enough to get back underground."

The guards touched down on the farthest end of the terrace as Cerberus began to sniff around the edges. "No one move!" they shouted.

But their order seemed to have the opposite effect as

spirits at the front of the line hurriedly dove into the fountain and the line dashed forward.

"I think we're going to make it," Euri whispered.

Jack raised his head to see how far they were from the fountain when he suddenly spotted a familiar spirit in line ahead of them. He ducked behind Cora.

"What?" she asked.

"That's the ghost who knows me as the Living Avenger," he whispered, pointing to a small, stout African American woman in a gray flannel dress. "She saw me the night we were hanging out with the Latin Club at the Pinetum."

"Well, don't stare at her then," said Euri.

Jack looked away. "Anyway, we have the clue. Viele said we'll find epiphany in Seneca."

"What's Seneca?" asked Euri.

"Not what," said Jack. "Who. He's a Roman playwright and philosopher."

"*Facilius per partes in cognitionem totius adducimur,*" Cora recited.

"'We are more easily led part by part to an understanding of the whole,'" Jack translated. "He also held up the Central Park map. Maybe one of Seneca's sayings reveals a clue on the map? When we get back underground we should find a copy of his writings."

"The New York Public Library has secret storage beneath Bryant Park," Euri offered.

But Cora looked skeptical. "I don't know. Reading through all of Seneca's writings could take days. Maybe Seneca is something on the map."

"Well, it would have to be something unmarked," Jack said as he studied it. "Something that would have had a name but that Viele wouldn't have bothered recording. . . ." His gaze fell on the scattering of squares. "Cora, where's the Pinetum?"

A guard shouted angrily and the line lurched forward again. Cora gave him a perplexed look. She studied the map and then pointed. "Around Eighty-fourth Street."

"Right near the squares," said Jack with a grin. "Come on."

Euri looked alarmed. "Where are we going?"

"To ask one of the squatters if her camp had a name," he said. And then, before they could say anything else, he floated ahead and cut back into the line behind the ghost in the gray flannel dress. Euri and Cora dashed after him. The guards were advancing and Jack knew he didn't have much time. He leaned forward so that his mouth was close to the little ghost's white bonnet. "I promise I won't hurt you," he whispered in her ear. "But the guards are here, so please don't scream."

The little ghost swung around and her eyes bulged as she took in Jack.

"It's okay," said Euri. "He's with us."

But the ghost did not look reassured. Her eyes darted from Cora to Jack.

"I just died," Cora explained feebly.

"Please don't give us away," Jack whispered. "We just have a question, then we'll leave you alone."

"But you're the Living—" she began to stammer.

"Don't say it aloud. My name is Jack. I'm sorry that I shouted at you before. What's your name?"

The ghost hesitated. She still looked as if she might be moments away from giving them up. Jack hoped he had made the right decision. The guards were getting closer as Cerberus began to howl.

"Jack, hurry!" said Cora.

The ghost stared at her with wide-eyes. "I'm Aurora," she said uncertainly.

Jack smiled at her. "You're one of the squatters who lived here before it became the park, right?"

Aurora jerked back in surprise and her dark eyes flashed indignantly. "I'm no squatter!"

Jack glanced helplessly at Cora and Euri. Aurora had been haunting the Pinetum, which was part of the area where the squatters had been. Her clothes looked like what someone would wear in the nineteenth century. And she was African American. But his guess was clearly wrong. "Sorry," he said, his head hanging down. "I'll leave you—"

But Aurora didn't seem to hear him. "We lived there rightfully!" she continued. "In Seneca Village!"

Jack jerked his head up as Cora gasped. He pulled out the map and pointed to the squares. "This was Seneca Village?"

Aurora nodded.

"I guess it has nothing to do with that Roman guy," said Euri.

Aurora studied Euri with obvious annoyance. "Several of us read *Seneca's Morals*," she retorted. "We weren't squatters, though. We bought that land—all of us! Epiphany Davis bought his lots all the way back in 1825. There are deeds to prove it. The city had us evicted."

"Did you just say Epiphany?" asked Cora.

"Yes, Epiphany Davis."

"Where can we find him?" Jack asked.

Aurora peered at them skeptically. "What do you want with Epiphany?"

"I didn't just die," Cora admitted. "I'm still alive and so is Jack, and we're stuck here in the underworld. But my mother is sick and I need to get back to her. Someone said he'd be able to help us."

Aurora's face softened. "He's gone back underground for the day, but at night he haunts Summit Rock," she said pointing toward the jagged rock-covered hill north of them. "Part of the village was there, too. We weren't squatters though—he'll tell you."

"I think we got that part," Euri remarked.

Aurora glared at Euri and jabbed at the map. "Don't those look like buildings to you?" she said, her voice rising. "There were three churches. A school. But what did the rich care? They wanted this park. A bunch of free blacks and poor white folk weren't going to stop them."

"Shhh!" Euri pleaded.

But it was too late. With a loud bark from all three of his heads, Cerberus scampered toward them.

"Over there!" shouted the guards.

The ghosts near the front of the line began to stampede forward.

Euri and Jack grabbed Cora's hands and shoved through the crowd. Elbowing several ghosts aside, they flew over the rim of the fountain and jumped in.

XXVI | A Secret Revealed

Before Jack and Cora even hit the tunnel floor, Euri was dragging them forward.

"What's the rush?" a spirit in a Yankees cap grumbled before a loud bark cut him off. He shrank back as Cerberus and a pair of guards bounded past him.

Ghosts began to scream and push each other out of the way as Euri shoved through the crowd. "The Dynamo Room," she said, brushing past a hysterical ghost in a sequined evening gown who was blocking her way. "The guards don't know about that."

She turned down a corridor lined with sweating pipes, but Cerberus, who had picked up their scent, barreled after them. "We won't have time to take the elevator," Euri added.

Jack turned back just as Cerberus bared all three heads' worth of teeth. "Just get us out of here!"

Euri darted around a corner and they sailed through a

metal door. Jack expected her to keep flying, but instead they began to fall, dropping through an elevator shaft. Cora opened her mouth to scream, but Jack clamped his free hand over it. With a pop, they dropped through the top of the elevator. They were inside the elevator for barely a moment before they tumbled out the bottom of it and continued to fall. As the elevator shot up over their heads, Euri finally slowed them down. After drifting to the bottom, they staggered through the wall of the shaft and collapsed on the floor of the Dynamo Room.

"We made it," panted Jack.

Euri shook her head sadly and pointed at Cora's shoe-less foot. "Not the sneaker."

Cora laughed. "It died for a good cause. Our Epiphany is in Seneca *Village*! You did it, Jack!"

"It was nothing," Jack said awkwardly, blushing. But he felt, in fact, like Seneca Village was everything. He had made a promise to Cora, and now he could keep it. He wouldn't fail her the way he'd failed Euri. "Tomorrow night we'll go find Epiphany at Summit Rock," he said. "He'll get us back."

"But first we need to look for Austin," Cora said. "We need to take him with us."

Jack had forgotten about Austin. For a moment, he wished that Cora had forgotten about him as well. "Of course," he said.

"I know we'll find him," Cora said. "I can't wait to get out of here!"

Euri stood and began to float back to the elevator shaft.

"Where are you going?" Jack asked.

Euri didn't turn back. "I need to visit some friends."

Jack knew she was lying, but he didn't try to stop her. He could tell she wanted to be alone.

Cora watched her float through the shaft wall. "I shouldn't have said that about being glad to get out of here."

"It's just hard for her that we're leaving," he explained.

Cora stared at him thoughtfully. "And yet she helped us. She cares about you, Jack."

He looked away. "Come on," he said, pulling Cora to her feet and floating with her to the office. "We should get some sleep."

Cora squeezed his hand. "I don't know if I can."

Jack wasn't sure if he could, either. He wanted to tell Cora how he felt about her. It seemed like the perfect time. But he couldn't help thinking about Euri and what Cora had said. He cared about Euri, too, but she had to understand that he needed to be with a girl who could change and grow, a living girl, a girl like Cora. If he could bring Euri back to life, maybe things would be different. But he couldn't. It would be pointless to love Euri.

Once they reached the office, Cora flopped onto the dirty floor. "I really had given up."

Jack sat down next to her. "I wasn't going to let you die."

Cora sat up. "I know, Jack. You've been wonderful. Thank you."

He looked her straight in the eye. "I wasn't going to let you die because . . ."

"Because you promised. I know."

Jack took a deep breath. "No. Because I like you."

Cora smiled but it wasn't the smile that Jack was expecting. It was a sympathetic smile, as if he had just told her he had a fatal disease. He felt his face turn red.

She put her hand gently on his. "I know you do."

Jack cringed. Had he been so obvious?

"And you're such a great friend," Cora continued.

Jack couldn't help the flash of hurt in his voice. "But—?"

"But . . . I feel terrible, Jack, but I like someone else."

There was an awkward silence.

"I'm sorry," she said.

He pulled his hand away. "That's okay," he heard a voice that sounded like his own say. "It's Austin."

Cora nodded. "He doesn't know," she added. "Or at least I don't think he does."

Jack couldn't help himself. "Why him?"

"I don't know. I've liked him for a really long time. He's always comfortable with himself. He doesn't take anything too seriously. He belongs at Chapman."

"So do you," said Jack. "You belong better than I do."

"I belong in Latin Club," she said with a smile. "I really care about you, Jack. I do. And I should have told you about my mom. You're my *amicus usque ad aram*."

Friend to the death, Jack translated to himself.

"And even after," she added.

"Sure," said his voice. He was glad it sounded steady and detached. "I guess we better get some rest."

Cora turned on her side and closed her eyes. He guessed she was just pretending to be asleep so she wouldn't have to talk to him. But eventually her breathing changed and Jack realized she really was asleep. He felt relieved that she was no longer conscious, then angry that she had been able to fall asleep so quickly.

But as he lay there, Jack realized that the person he really hated was Austin. Every time Cora talked about him, she became someone different than the girl he thought she was—someone more insecure, more like Jack himself. And Austin was comfortable with himself because he had been born wealthy and Chapman was practically his home. He hadn't earned any of these things. Jack thought about how Austin had made fun of the flowers he had given Cora, and how he'd always ignored him at school. Even in the underworld, he had ignored Jack—

going his own way and making everything more complicated. Jack briefly imagined taking Cora back and leaving Austin to die. But when he looked at Cora, he knew he could never go through with it.

He rested his head on his knees and envisioned Cora and Austin holding hands around school. The line from the Auden poem popped into his head: "'Let the more loving one be me,'" he whispered into the empty space between his knees. The poet had been dead wrong about that—loving someone who didn't love you back was the worst situation to be in, the loneliest . . .

"You're not sleeping."

Jack looked up. Euri had floated through the office door and was hovering in front of him.

"I'm not tired," he said.

"Mourning sickness?"

He felt her studying him and turned away. "No, I'm fine."

"Okay. Let's be fine together."

After a moment of silence, Jack glanced over at her, floating glumly next to him. He caught her eye and they both grinned.

"What's wrong?" asked Euri.

Jack looked at Cora, who was snoring softly. "She likes someone else."

"Who? Austin?"

Jack didn't want to tell Euri the truth. "No, just this guy at school."

Euri dug into her blazer pocket. "Where does he live? I may have an extra cockroach in here somewhere."

Jack smiled. "That's okay."

"Don't worry. You'll find someone else," said Euri, patting his hand.

The way she touched his hand reminded Jack of the way Cora had done it, as if he was a small child and they were adults. "You didn't."

Euri grimaced. "What are you talking about?"

"I mean Nate. He must have been the one with you when you jumped. Who is he, Euri?"

"You just told me who he is."

"No, I mean why was he there when you jumped in front of the train? Did you jump because of him?"

Euri froze. "We were supposed to jump together," she finally said.

Jack felt a chill run up his spine. "Why?"

"Nate's parents didn't want us seeing each other anymore. I loved him."

"Why didn't you just run away together? Why did . . . you know?"

"I don't know," Euri snapped. "I was depressed and it was a stupid idea, okay? He realized that. I didn't."

"But you said he was there."

Euri was picking at the hem of her skirt more aggressively than Jack had ever seen. "We held hands," she said in a muffled voice. "Then we stood on the edge of the platform. When we saw a train coming, we counted to three. On three, I jumped. He let go of my hand. . . ." Tears began to slide down her cheeks.

"He didn't jump?"

Euri shook her head. A dark look crossed her face as she wiped at the tears with her sleeve. "I'm never going to stop haunting him."

"Why did you start?" he asked. "You didn't haunt him last time I was here."

"No," Euri admitted. "I started after you left."

"Why?" He couldn't stop himself. "You're not planning to move on, are you?"

"Never!" said Euri fiercely.

Jack closed his eyes, feeling relieved and then quickly guilty. Euri wanted him to make it back to the living world. Didn't he want her to be at peace?

"I just want him to suffer," she continued, her pale blue eyes narrowing.

"But you can't blame him for not killing himself—"

"I can do whatever I want," Euri said indignantly. "I'm the dead one. You're about to go back to the living world. You can do whatever you want, grow up, have a life. You'll find another girl."

She was admitting the very thing Jack had wanted her to understand—that he was alive and she wasn't. But now, he no longer believed it himself. "I'm a freak, Euri. You said it yourself. I'm barely alive. I don't even know who I am. I see ghosts in the living world, I fly in the dead one."

"Well, that's who you are, then."

"But I want to be like everyone else. Not some freak."

"If you weren't some freak, you wouldn't see me. We wouldn't be friends." Euri put her arms around him and Jack hugged her back. He suddenly felt he couldn't bear to leave her. She read the hesitation in his face. "Promise me you're going to go back tomorrow?"

He sniffed. "I promised already."

"You're so brave down here. Now just be brave up there."

"I'll try." He closed his eyes, feeling tired for the first time that morning. Minutes later, he was asleep.

XXVII | The Search Party

"It's almost sunset."

Jack slowly opened his eyes. Euri was standing beside him. He yawned and stretched, then looked at Cora, who was still asleep. He felt awkward about their conversation and almost didn't want to wake her up. But Euri had already floated over to her and was poking her arm. "Cora, wake up, it's time to go."

Cora opened her eyes and sat up, looking momentarily confused before she caught sight of Jack and smiled.

"We better go find Austin," he said, unable to look her in the eye.

Euri reached out and took Cora's hand and he hurried ahead of them, flying quickly, so he wouldn't have to take Cora's other hand.

Soon they burst out of Bethesda Fountain and into a nippy night. A cold wind rustled through the trees, scattering dry brown leaves onto the terrace and blowing them into the lake. As the lamps around the terrace switched on, Jack looked wistfully at the arcs of ghosts zooming toward the city. In contrast, the living, wearing jackets and emitting little puffs of air, seemed weighed down.

"We should start by flying to all the places where we saw Austin before," Euri said. "We need to be careful, though. I heard a spirit counter tell someone that the Living Threat Level's been raised again."

Jack didn't know what to say to Cora, so he didn't say anything. Instead, he tried to look busy searching for Austin, craning his neck for guards and dipping away from Euri and Cora to search through clusters of ghosts. They checked around Bethesda Fountain, where Cora had first seen Austin. But they didn't see anyone who looked even remotely like him. Then they flew down to Trinity Church, where they zoomed up and down Broadway, calling his name. On the way back uptown, Jack realized that Euri was taking them up Ludlow Street. "What are we doing here?" he asked Euri as the familiar tenement came into view.

"I'm looking for Austin," Euri replied nonchalantly.

"Here?" asked Cora. "Why would he be here?"

"It might be on his route," said Euri with a shrug as they landed on Nate's fire escape.

"Or on *your* route," said Cora under her breath.

"This isn't exactly the best time to haunt," Jack agreed. He caught a glimpse through the window of Nate scribbling song lyrics on the wall.

"Fine," said Euri, turning around. She seemed disappointed. "Let's leave."

They flew up Avenue A to St. Mark's, where they searched the sidewalks outside St. Dymphna's Bar, Addiction NYC body piercing, and Chrysalis Acupuncture. But there was no sign of Austin.

Cora sighed. "He was in front of the comics store last time. Let's check inside."

But when they flew into St. Mark's Comics, all they found were several ghosts gathered to discuss Superman #80, "Superman's Lost Brother." None of them had seen Austin. Even Euri looked frustrated. "I suppose we could try his parents' apartment," she suggested.

It was just after 2 A.M. when they reached Austin's fancy apartment house on Central Park West. The Beresford was a hulking building overlooking the park and topped by three towers illuminated by large copper lanterns. "I think he lives in Apartment 16A," said Cora. As they flew up the side of the building, Jack tried to ignore the fact that Cora knew Austin's apartment number by heart.

They floated over a stone balcony and through a

window into an apartment that seemed to extend end-lessly with fireplaces, a formal dining room, and bedrooms as large as Jack's entire apartment. The halls were lined with oil portraits, including one of a plump man dressed in a white lab coat. "Hey, look," said Jack. "That's the ghost Austin was traveling with."

"Maybe that's his great-grandfather?" said Cora. "The one who worked on the Manhattan Project?"

"He must be," said Jack, thinking of how he had first seen him haunting the Columbia tunnels.

"At least he's with family," said Cora.

There was also a portrait of Austin and his brother, a chubby, older, dark-eyed boy, holding hands when they were small. Euri floated in front of it, staring intensely at the boys' faces.

"I wonder how he died," Cora said, leaning in to peer at Austin's brother. "Poor Austin."

But Jack didn't feel like Austin needed much sympathy. One vast bedroom was filled with musical equipment—amplifiers, keyboards, and drum sets. Another was a mess of lacrosse sticks, comic books, and Chapman banners from different years. There was a cigar-tinged library with leather furniture and floor-to-ceiling volumes of Latin texts, though Jack also noticed some English poetry and a first edition of *The Lord of the Rings*. The elevator doors were entirely brass and had a crested

shield of a dragon and a bear with the motto FRONTE
NULLA FIDES—*Place no trust in appearances.* This seemed like
a joke. Watching Cora's eyes take in the luxurious sur-
roundings, Jack knew he could never compete.

"It doesn't look like anyone is home," said Euri.
"Come on, it's after midnight. We don't want to miss
Epiphany."

Jack felt secretly relieved.

"We can't just let Austin die!" Cora said.

"I wouldn't worry about Austin," said Euri, pointing at
Cora's hands. "I would worry about you."

They all looked at Cora's hands, which had turned a
paler shade than the rest of her, revealing the blue veins
beneath.

Cora turned to Jack. "What's happening?"

"Your body is starting to feel the effects of being in
the underworld." Jack studied his own hands. They still
looked solid. "I guess it takes mine a little longer. But
Euri's right. We better start looking for Epiphany. Half
the night is already over."

Cora gazed longingly around the apartment, her eyes
coming to rest on the portrait of the two brothers.

"I'll keep looking for Austin," Euri offered. "But it
would be foolish for you to wait any longer."

Still, Cora hesitated. Jack tried the one thing he
knew that would make her leave. "You need to get back

to your mom. She can't take care of herself without you."

A tear ran down Cora's cheek as she nodded and took his hand.

XXVIII | The Return of the Living Avenger

As they flew across Central Park West and into the park, Jack wondered if Cora could learn to love him. It wasn't his fault, after all, that Austin had run off to find his brother and didn't want to be found. He knew his tiny three-room apartment was a far cry from the Beresford, but perhaps eventually—after Cora recovered from Austin's death—she would consider visiting Jack there. He would slowly impress her with funny Latin expressions and stories from his father's archaeological digs, and one day, she would realize that it was he she had liked all along.

As they circled the elevated outcrop of Summit Rock, Jack noticed that several ghosts in nineteenth-century outfits were hovering over it, some talking in tight circles, others quietly surveying the park alone.

"There's Aurora," said Euri, pointing to a ghost in a gray flannel dress floating above a bench at the top of the ridge.

As Jack flew toward her, Aurora looked up, her expression startled, then cross. "Cerberus nearly took a bite out of me," she grumbled as he touched down in front of her.

"Well, it was your own fault for shouting," said Euri.

"Sorry about that," Jack said. "Is Epiphany here?"

"Epiphany!" Aurora yelled, waving at the other side of the rock.

A thin ghost with a stubbly face and dark, hooded eyes floated over to them. From the way he looked at Cora, Jack could tell that he recognized she was alive.

"These children think you can help them," said Aurora.

"We're looking for a way back to the living world," said Jack. "We heard there's one in Seneca Village. That you would know."

Epiphany shook his head. "I don't know about any such thing."

Jack saw the worried look on Cora's face. They had both been so excited about figuring out Viele's clue that they hadn't considered whether his information was accurate. Perhaps it was outdated and the secret way out had disappeared years earlier? Or perhaps Viele had lied?

Aurora put her hand on Cora's shoulder. "This child's mother is sick."

"Please," Cora pleaded. "I need to get back to her."

Epiphany's dark eyes latched on to Cora's. "Who sent you?"

"Viele," said Cora. "The mapmaker."

At the mention of Viele's name, Epiphany spat on the ground.

"Viele was happy to see us go," Aurora explained. "He called us squatters, too."

"You're pretty sensitive about that," said Euri.

"We have reason to be," said Epiphany. "We were landowners. We had a community. All of it was taken away because of who we were."

"I think maybe Viele regrets that now," said Jack. "He didn't say anything bad about you."

"He did do us one good turn," Epiphany admitted. "But not because he respected us. We had a common enemy."

Jack thought about the park's designers, the ones Viele had sued. "Olmsted and Vaux?"

Epiphany nodded. "Seneca Village had a spring. It's where we got our fresh water. The city took everything away from us when they built the park. But we didn't let them take the spring. When they destroyed our homes, we hid it.

"Viele knew about the spring from his surveying. He disliked us but he hated the park's designers even more, so he kept our secret. It's not on his map."

He looked at Jack. "But there's one thing you should know. It only works if you're alive."

Jack thought about what Viele had told him. He was alive if he chose to be. "I am alive."

"And he needs to go back," said Euri firmly.

"My mistake," Epiphany said, peering at him more closely. "There was something dead about you."

"So you'll take us?" said Cora.

"As long as you remember us when you get back to the living world," said Epiphany. "Remember what was here."

"Of course we will!" said Jack.

"We'll tell everyone we know about Seneca," added Cora.

For the first time since they'd met him, Epiphany smiled. "Follow me."

Aurora waved good-bye as they flew after him down a sloping trail that descended the south side of Summit Rock. Behind them, they could hear the shouts of ghost children at the playground. Across the wall dividing the park from Central Park West, Jack could see the Beresford. He quickly turned away, trying not to think about Austin. His fate was sealed, Jack told himself. At least he would be with his great-grandfather and brother.

Epiphany led them off the path to an area at the base of Summit Rock that was covered with dry leaves and rocks. He took a branch and poked around the ground. "Sometimes even I have a hard time finding it," he said.

A moment later, he grunted. "Here it is."

Jack looked at the dry, gray rock at Epiphany's feet. It didn't look like a spring at all.

"That's it?" asked Cora.

Epiphany carefully looked around, and then picked up the rock and moved it away. Behind it, trickled a small spring. "This will bring you back to the living world," he said. "Just step into it. Quickly now."

Cora turned to Euri and threw her arms around her in a big hug. Euri stiffened, surprised, then hugged her back, resting her head on Cora's shoulder.

"I'm sorry you can't come back with us," Cora said.

Only Jack saw the tears gather in Euri's eyes. She blinked furiously, holding them back as she let go of Cora and straightened up. "You shouldn't have worried about getting back. Jack doesn't break his promises."

"Neither do you," Cora said.

Euri smiled.

"If you see Austin, tell him—" Cora hesitated. "Tell him I'll miss him."

"Hurry," Epiphany said. "We don't want any of the guards to discover us."

Jack knew it was his turn to say good-bye to Euri. "Come see me this time?"

"As long as I can stay out of Bloomingdale," she said, not quite looking him in the eye.

He felt he should hug her but he was afraid he would cry. He let go of her hand and took Cora's. "We better go," he said, stepping toward the spring.

Suddenly, Aurora flew toward them. In her hand she held a newspaper, which she waved in the air. "Special edition of the *Underworld Times!*" she said. "Mann Down is reporting that the guards have the Living Avenger in custody!"

"But that's impossible," said Cora.

"That's what I thought," said Aurora, eyeing Jack.

"That column is nothing but lies," said Euri crossly. "Go."

But Jack was curious. "Do they have a picture of him?"

"No picture of him," Aurora said.

"See, it's just made up," said Euri.

"All they have is a picture of the weapon he was carrying," said Aurora.

"The weapon?" said Jack.

Aurora held out the paper. As soon as Jack saw the photo, a sickened feeling came over him. It was his pouch of ghost repellent. There was only one way the guards could have gotten it. His mind began to race. He could step into the spring with Cora. They would both be safe.

"Jack," Cora gasped, an alarmed look on her face. "That's not the pouch you gave Austin—?"

But, before she could finish, he pushed her into the spring, taking care not to get his own feet wet. Cora stumbled onto the glistening rock and vanished into the ground.

XXIX | The Tomb Raiders

"What are you doing?" asked Euri. "Are you crazy?"

For a moment, Jack thought he was.

"You'll never rescue him! There are only a couple hours left till dawn." Euri grabbed his arm. "Jack's going to go, too," she explained to Epiphany. She turned back to him. "You promised!"

Jack shook his head. "I need to get Austin first."

Euri crossed her arms over her chest. "But he's the guy that Cora likes."

Jack didn't answer.

"I'll go after him," said Euri. "You go back."

"No," said Jack.

"Why are you doing this?"

"I don't know," said Jack.

"She won't choose you just for saving him."

"I know!" said Jack, trying to keep the anger out of his voice. "I can't compete. He's Austin Chapman, the richest, most popular guy in the whole school."

Euri grabbed his arm and started shoving him toward the spring. "Forget it! It's not worth risking your life for him."

But Jack held his ground. "Can I come back later tonight?" he asked Epiphany.

"You're one strange living person," Epiphany observed. "But the spring will still be here. Just make sure you're not being followed."

Jack turned to Aurora. "Does the story say where the guards might have taken him?"

Aurora began reading from the paper. " 'Inspector Stephen Kennedy wants to reassure the public that the Living Avenger has been apprehended. "An accomplice escaped, but we have the Avenger himself in custody at The Tombs," the Inspector revealed early this morning to Mann Down.' "

"The Tombs?" said Jack. "Is that a cemetery?"

"It's a suicide mission," Euri grumbled.

Jack grinned. "Well, luckily, you're already dead."

Fifteen minutes later, as they floated over a packed parking lot across from the courthouse, Euri pointed to a bridge one story above the ground, with frosted glass windows connecting 100 Centre Street to a drab, concrete tower. "That's the Bridge of Sighs," she explained. "Prisoners cross it to go between the courthouse and the Tombs. It's not a cemetery, Jack, it's a jail."

The Tombs reminded Jack of a very tall and sinister parking garage. A slender frosted glass window ran the length of it and slivers of unnaturally bright light leaked out through narrow windows embedded in the thick layers of gray concrete. The bottom stories had no windows at all—just black vents—and the very top seemed to be a lattice of bars. "Why is it called the Tombs?" he asked.

"Professor Schmitt . . ." Euri paused.

Jack put his hand on her arm. "I'm sorry, Euri."

"I don't know why he was in such a hurry to move on," she snapped.

Taking a hundred and fifty years didn't seem like much of a hurry, but Jack nodded sympathetically.

Euri sighed. "He once told me that the original building looked a lot like an Egyptian tomb. I guess the name just stuck."

"Have you ever been inside?"

Euri looked mildly offended. "Do I look like a criminal?" Then she frowned. "Don't answer that. They don't lock up juvenile offenders anyway—unless, I guess, they're alive. They just send them to Bloomingdale."

"How do they lock up ghosts." Jack asked. "Can't they just fly right out?"

"The haunters can. But the ones who've violated underworld rules have to wear ankle charms. If they tried to leave, the guards can just track them down."

Jack studied the building. "It looks like it has a lot of cells. I wonder where Austin—"

"Forget Austin," Euri pleaded. "Let's just go back to the spring. You promised me you'd go back."

"And I will," he said. "But first I need to get—"

"Austin, Austin, Austin!" Euri shrieked. "He wouldn't do the same for you!"

"Shhh!" whispered Jack, looking around the dark parking lot. A rat scampered out from under a car and into an alley. He continued in a quiet voice. "Maybe he wouldn't. But I'm going inside. If you don't want to come, don't."

He flew across the street and toward the Bridge of Sighs without looking back. Slipping through the frosted glass window, he found himself in an enclosed walkway with buzzing fluorescent lighting. Three living men in scruffy clothes and with downcast eyes shuffled through him as corrections officers escorted them toward the courthouse. Ahead he could hear the buzz of a security door as it opened and another living prisoner was escorted out.

Flying through it, he entered a broad hall that echoed with shouts, moans, and eerie bursts of laughter from above. Looking up, Jack saw several floors of cell blocks, stacked one atop the other.

"Who are you?"

Jack started. A dead guard was floating in the shadows, glaring at him.

"I work for Mann Down," Jack stuttered. "I'm reporting on the Living Avenger."

"He's not taking interviews."

"Can I just take a look around?" Jack asked. "Just so I can describe the building?"

"You're not supposed to . . ."

"It's my first day on the job," Jack pleaded. "If I come back empty-handed—"

The guard waved Jack up. "I didn't see nothing."

As Jack floated up, he noticed that the tiny cells were crammed with both the living and the dead, though it was hard to tell who seemed more distraught. A few of the living prisoners slept, their faces pale and twitching under the fluorescent light, but many others hung on to the bars, shouting, weeping, laughing hysterically or simply staring out with haunted eyes. The dead prisoners cursed, moaned, and generally added to the overall feeling of gloom and hopelessness. But unlike the living ones, they occasionally floated out of their cells to spread their misery to other floors.

As he drifted around the first level, Jack peered into each cell.

"Who you looking for, sonny?" cackled a leering ghost dressed in dirty petticoats.

"They left me in here with the rats!" shouted a bow-legged spirit with gaping holes in his face.

Jack shuddered and continued to the next floor and a new row of cell blocks. The first cell looked dark and empty, but just as Jack was about to float away, what he had thought was a pile of rags burst up from the floor. "Stand ho! Who goes there?" it roared in a sonorous British accent.

Jack jumped backward. The spirit arched his thick eyebrows in a dramatic way, waiting for an answer.

But before Jack could say anything, a voice from above suddenly shouted, "No more Hamlet!"

"'All that lives must die, passing through nature to eternity!'" the spirit roared back, rolling his r's so they trilled and echoed across the prison.

"For crying out loud," the ghost above howled, "we know!"

The spirit ignored this outburst and, grabbing Jack by the collar, stage-whispered into his ear. "Junius Brutus Booth, tragedian."

"And drunk," shouted the ghost from above. "They'd lock him up here between performances."

"Jack," said Jack, gently loosening Booth's powerful grip on his collar. Booth's name was familiar. "You're not related to the man who shot President Lincoln?"

"He's the traitor's father!" the ghost from above said.

At this, Booth hung his head and his translucent brown eyes filled with tears. "'It is a wise father that knows his own child,'" he said in a quavering voice.

"Um, sorry for asking," Jack whispered so the ghost above wouldn't hear. Booth started to weep. "I'd better be going," said Jack awkwardly. But this only made Booth sob harder. Jack hesitated, afraid he would alert the guards.

"I thought you were going to find Austin!"

Jack spun around. Euri was floating behind him with her arms crossed.

"You came!" Jack whispered.

She glowered at him but her lips twitched, and Jack could tell she was fighting a smile.

Booth instantly brightened. "Behold Pyramus and Thisbe!"

Euri eyed him wearily. "What's this old coot talking about?"

"Characters from the play in *A Midsummer Night's Dream*," Jack explained. "They're lovers separated by a wall. It's based on a myth in Ovid—"

"I don't think we have time for English class," Euri interrupted in a tense voice. She turned to Booth. "Where's the living boy? Where are they keeping him?"

Booth cocked his head. "The next floor up," he whispered, "on the other side of the block. Malachi Fallon, the warden, is guarding him personally."

"I was just about to ask him that," said Jack.

"Right," said Euri, grabbing his hand and pulling him down the corridor.

As they floated up toward the top level of cells, Jack turned to Euri. "If the warden is guarding him, how are we . . . ?"

"I don't know," said Euri, touching down on a quiet floor of mostly empty cells. "We need to eyeball where he is first and figure it out. At least he won't have an ankle charm. Since he's alive, the bars really hold him."

"But this isn't the top floor," said Jack.

"I know. It's the one beneath it." She floated up to the ceiling, and her head disappeared through the cement. With one hand, she waved him up to do the same.

Jack flew up and shoved his head hard against the concrete, which reluctantly gave, as if he were putting on a very tight sweater. As soon as his head popped up through the floor, Euri turned to him and put her finger to her lips. Close by, they could hear a familiar voice, crisp and precise, asking questions.

"How long have you been terrorizing the underworld?" demanded Inspector Kennedy.

"I don't know what you're talking about," said a tired-sounding voice.

"Austin!" Jack mouthed.

"I know your type, son," Kennedy mused. "Full of sob stories. Tough family life. No one loves you. Well, the law doesn't care. If you value your miserable life, *Living Avenger*, answer the question."

Jack's heart pounded in his chest. The sob story was his. He was the one who should rightfully be locked up.

"I told you," said Austin, his voice cracking, "I don't know what you're talking about."

"Let me have a go at him, governor," said a man's eager voice in an Irish brogue.

"Very well, Fallon," said Kennedy with a sigh. "But don't kill him. His time will be up soon enough, and in the meantime, I want him alive."

Footsteps began to echo toward them as they ducked back down through the floor.

"They must be just a couple of cells in that direction," whispered Euri, pointing to the left. She grabbed Jack's hand, dragging him twenty feet down the cell block and then popped her head back up through the ceiling.

When Jack joined her, he found himself looking through thick bars into a dim cell. In a corner of the cell, a figure sat on the floor, rocking back and forth, his hair disheveled. Above him stood a ghost wearing a black cravat and holding Jack's ghost-repellent pouch with the tips of his fingers. He had a low, heavy brow and droopy eyes.

"So, boy, are you sure this isn't your weapon?"

"Weapon?" Austin said. "Someone gave it to me for allergies."

"You can't keep on lying to us."

"I'm not! Just leave me alone!"

Fallon snickered. "Well, Mr. Avenger, you're in luck today," he said. Without waiting for Austin to ask him why, he smiled. "A prominent newspaper columnist has expressed his concern for your health and well-being."

Jack exchanged worried glances with Euri.

"He promised me something if I gave you this." Fallon put the ghost-repellent pouch on the floor and then dug around in his pocket. "Ah, here it is." He held out his arm and offered Austin the same chocolate bonbon that Colonel Mann had offered Cora.

Ever since Auden had explained the derivation of Cora's name, Jack had been worried that she would eat something and die, just like *Kore*. But with a sickening feeling, he realized that it wasn't Cora who shared Proserpina's fate—it was Austin.

Fallon continued to dangle the chocolate in front of him. "Come now, boy, you must be hungry," he cooed. "And if you want to stay alive, you need to keep up your strength."

As if in a dream, Jack watched Austin stick out his hand and take the candy.

"Best you ever tasted," said Fallon with a laugh.

Austin held the chocolate up and studied it, as if about to take a bite.

XXX | Austin's Secret

Euri grabbed his arm. "I'll distract Fallon. You get Austin. Don't wait for me. We'll meet back at the spring."

Before Jack could say anything, she flew up through the floor, into the cell, and toward the warden. At the sight of her, Austin dropped the chocolate. Fallon just looked annoyed.

"I have a message from Colonel Mann," she said.

"I'm in the middle of doing his bidding," Fallon griped. "And since when does he hire schoolgirls?"

Euri crossed her arms. "Since when does he hire corrupt wardens?"

Fallon bristled.

"Go ahead and ignore me, but the colonel won't be happy." With a flounce of her skirt, Euri turned to go.

"Wait!" Fallon croaked.

But Euri had already floated out of the cell and down the row of cell blocks. Fallon flew after her. She slowed to talk to him, but Jack could no longer hear what they were saying. All he knew was that the conversation wasn't going to last long. He flew through the bars and up to Austin, kicking the chocolate out of his reach. "We're going to get you out of here," he said.

He expected Austin to leap to his feet, but he made no move to get up.

"Come on," whispered Jack. "We have to go."

But Austin just laughed.

"What's wrong with you?" said Jack.

"I'm crazy," Austin explained. "I'm hanging out with my dead great-grandfather. I'm seeing you and Cora flying around." He shuddered. "And then there's—"

"You're not crazy. You're just in the underworld." Jack tugged on his arm, but Austin refused to budge.

"That's what my great-grandfather said. But I told him he's just a hallucination."

Jack looked anxiously at Fallon, but thankfully, he was still talking to Euri, his back turned. "Did you find your brother?"

Austin looked confused. "My brother?"

"We figured that's why you ran off. He's dead, right?"

"No," said Austin, with a grin. "He's crazy, too."

Jack wished that Cora could see Austin now, his hair greasy, his eyes darting around. Being in the Tombs had clearly affected his sanity. But then Jack reminded himself that it was his own fault that Austin was there and he needed to save him. Austin's hands, like Cora's, were beginning to turn a cadaverous pale color, and Fallon was bound to turn back around at any second. Jack picked up the ghost-repellent pouch and stuck it in his pocket. "We're going," he said as he dragged Austin to his feet and pulled him through the bars.

"Help!" Austin shouted.

Jack clapped his hand over Austin's mouth, but it was too late. Fallon turned and began to fly toward them, yelling, "Guards! Guards!"

"Go through the ceiling!" Euri shouted from the other end of the cell block.

"Traitor!" Fallon howled at her.

Jack could see guards fly in from every direction and surround Euri.

"Get her to Bloomingdale!" Fallon ordered. "And the rest of you, catch the Living Avenger and that ghost accomplice!"

As the guards seized Euri under the arms, Jack knew that there was nothing he could do to help her. He had to get Austin to the spring before the guards caught them, too. He rocketed up into the air, holding Austin's hand in a firm grip as they sailed through the latticework of iron bars and burst into the night.

Jack looked over his shoulder. Two guards were right behind them. He weaved around several buildings and then dove down into an alley, pulling Austin behind a Dumpster. Austin opened his mouth, but this time Jack clapped his hand over it in time.

"We lost them!" one of the guards shouted from above.

"We need Cerberus," said another. "He'll smell the Avenger."

"Come on, let's get him," said the first.

After waiting a moment to be sure the guards had left, Jack released his hand from Austin's mouth and pulled him back up into air. "What's the matter with you?" he nearly shouted as they raced over Broadway toward Central Park. "Are you trying to kill us?!"

"She's been chasing after me," Austin said. "And you're helping her!"

"Cora's not chasing after you," said Jack. "She just likes you."

"Not Cora. Deirdre!"

Jack almost crashed into the side of a building. "Deirdre?"

"I knew I was going crazy from the moment I saw her. She's haunting me. Just like—"

Everything suddenly became clear. "Nate," Jack whispered. "Your brother."

Austin nodded, his eyes feverish.

Jack looked at Austin, amazed that he had known Euri when she was alive.

"And you're trying to haunt me, too," Austin charged.

"Me?"

"You fly around with her. You must be dead. Did you kill yourself, too?"

"I'm not dead!" Jack snapped. "And I didn't kill myself."

Austin bit his lip, which Jack noticed was turning a worrisome bluish color. "I'm sorry. I'm crazy. I know I'm crazy."

Jack couldn't believe that this was the same Austin who Cora—and just about everyone else at Chapman—idolized. "You're not crazy," he told him firmly.

But Austin shook his head. "When Nate started to lose it, he dropped out of college and moved to this disgusting apartment with cockroaches everywhere. He kept saying Deirdre was haunting him. I didn't tell anyone at school. I was embarrassed—but I was also worried the same thing was going to happen to me." Austin started to laugh. "I guess I don't have to worry about that anymore, though."

"The only thing you need to worry about is getting back to the living world before dawn," said Jack as they neared Seneca Village. Below, he could see the ghosts gathered on Summit Rock. He spotted Epiphany floating by himself and looking up at the night sky. Jack flew over to him.

"So you found him?" Epiphany said, eyeing Austin.

Jack nodded. He wished Euri could be there to say

good-bye to them. He hated to think of his last image of her, surrounded by guards. As they followed Epiphany down to the spring, Jack had the urge to ask Austin a question. "Did anyone ever tell you why Deirdre killed herself?"

Austin shook his head. "I was a little kid when it happened. My parents just said she was troubled. They said Nate tried to stop her."

Jack thought about Euri's version of the story. "Did you believe them?"

"For a while. But after he moved to that apartment, Nate told me he had been planning to jump with her, too. They made a suicide pact. That's why she was haunting him, he said. Because he didn't jump."

Epiphany looked around to make sure no one was watching and then moved the rock to reveal the tiny, gurgling spring. "Who's first?"

"He is," said Jack, guiding Austin by his elbow toward the spring. "But wait, why didn't he jump?"

Austin frowned.

"What is it?" Jack asked.

"He would have done it. He was crazy about Deirdre. But just when he was about to jump, he said he thought about me." Tears gathered in Austin's eyes.

Jack looked at Dylan Thomas's pocket watch. There was barely an hour left until dawn. "Listen to me. You're not crazy and neither is Nate."

Austin sniffed. "And why is that?"

"Deirdre really *is* haunting him."

Austin chuckled. "And you're really the Living Avenger, right?"

Jack smiled. "Go find Cora." Then he pushed Austin against the rock.

Austin turned to him with a hurt expression. "Why did you do . . . ?" he started to say. But before he could finish, he disappeared into the ground.

"Hurry now," said Epiphany.

But Jack hesitated. If the guards had taken Euri back to Bloomingdale, he might not see her again for months, even years. He thought about what Austin had told him. Euri deserved to know it, too.

"Go!" shouted Epiphany suddenly.

Jack turned around. A pair of guards—with Cerberus snapping and growling between them—was flying toward them.

"The spring! They've seen the spring!" Epiphany cried. "Go, child! This is your last chance!"

"I'm sorry," said Jack. "I can't."

XXXI | The More Loving One

Jack flew out of the park, and straight into the first building he saw. He floated through several apartments, past sleeping children, and into a kitchen where a cat's yellow eyes widened at the sight of him. As he continued through the west side of the building, he tried to convince himself that even if the spring had been compromised, he could still find another way out. The important thing was to find Euri.

The sky was beginning to lighten as he flew up Broadway, past H&H Bagels and Harry's Shoes, toward Columbia. There were hardly any living people out—just some sleepy looking college kids wandering out of the subway and a few deliverymen unloading produce from trucks idling in front of grocery stores. He flew over the iron Columbia University gates and onto the campus, which was crowded with ghosts carrying books or talking in groups. In front of the library was a big, bowl-shaped granite fountain. Jack landed on its rim and dove into it. A few moments later, he was spit back underground, out onto the floor of a familiar crumbling brick and stone-lined tunnel. A ghost with wild hair and a black T-shirt reading a book entitled *The Birth of Tragedy* counted him in on her clicker.

Jack flew down a crumbling corridor, sticking his head through doors and into various Bloomingdale classes—belly dancing, introductory embalming, method acting—but Euri wasn't in any of them. He raced around a corner and collided with another ghost. They both tumbled to the ground.

Jack immediately recognized the plump spirit. "You're Austin's great-grandfather! The one who worked on the Manhattan Project!"

"Sam Chapman," the ghost said. He looked panicked. "There's only a half hour left. But even if I get him out of the Tombs where do I go? There's no way out. There's nothing I can do—"

"Austin's safe," Jack interrupted, standing back up.

"What?"

"I got him back to the living world. He'll be okay."

A look of relief spread across the old man's face. "You must be Jack. Austin told me about you."

Jack squatted down and put his hands on the spirit's shoulders. "There was a ghost who also helped save him," said Jack. "A girl."

"Austin thought she was someone to be afraid of. He

was confused. He didn't know where he was."

"It's okay," said Jack. "She was a patient here and the guards just brought her back. I need to know where she is. I don't have much time."

"She's probably having her reassessment interview with Dr. Earle," Sam said, floating to his feet. "I'll take you to his office."

They hurried down the corridor together and turned onto another, skidding to a stop in front of a half-open door. Poking his head around it, Jack spotted Euri floating above a battered old couch. No one else appeared to be in the office.

"Dr. Earle isn't here yet," Sam whispered. "I'll try to delay him. Go."

Jack slipped inside and closed the door.

The moment she caught sight of him, Euri hurried over. "What are you doing here? Where's Austin?"

"I sent him back." He reached out his hand. "Come on, let's get you out of here."

Euri pointed to her leg and Jack suddenly noticed the charm bracelet strapped to her ankle. "I can't leave Bloomingdale. But forget about me. What about you? Jack, it's almost dawn!"

"I had to tell you something. About Nate."

"What could be this important?" Euri stiffened. "I don't care about him."

"Then why do you haunt him?"

"Because . . . Just go back to the spring, Jack." Euri's voice sounded weary. "What does Austin know about the whole thing anyway? He was just this little kid when it happened. . . ."

Euri's eyes went distant and Jack suddenly remembered how old she really was. This year she looked younger than him, but she really should have been a grown-up, finishing college, living in her own place, maybe working already. He couldn't give her that future back, but maybe he could give her something else.

"What's going to happen to you?" he asked.

She picked at her skirt. "Dr. Earle is going to ask me some dumb questions about why I escaped. Then he's going to ask me if I've changed my mind about moving on. And I'm going to tell him I still don't want to. Ever. That I just want to get out of here and—"

She didn't say what she wanted to do, but the angry way she twisted up her face told Jack enough. He gently touched her arm. "The reason Nate didn't jump had nothing to do with you."

"You've got to get back to the spring. Just forget it!"

But Jack refused to move. "He didn't want to leave Austin."

Euri studied his face. "How do you know?"

"Nate told Austin. He knows you're haunting him,

too. Though everyone else just thinks he's crazy."

Euri's lower lip quivered. "He's haunting *me*."

"You have to forgive him," Jack said softly.

"It's not so easy," Euri nearly shouted. "I'm losing everyone—Professor Schmitt, you—" She stopped and stared up at him.

Jack felt an ache in his stomach. "Euri, it's impossible for us."

"I know," she cried.

"I have to grow up."

"I know you do."

"At least Nate really loved you," said Jack. "He just didn't want to leave his little brother all alone. He needed to help him grow up and steal the girl I liked!"

He hadn't meant to sound so mad. But when Jack's eyes met Euri's, they both burst out laughing. Jack suddenly felt as if everything he had just said about having to grow up and move on was wrong. He could never laugh with any other girl like this. He wanted to stay with Euri.

Euri wiped her eyes. "You'd better get back to the spring."

He flashed a weak smile. "I can't."

"What do you mean you can't!?"

"The guards saw it. I can't go back that way."

"You got Austin through but you didn't go yourself!"

"I wanted to tell you about Nate. . . ."

"Jack! What did you do?" Euri grabbed his hand and pulled him toward the door. "We need to try and get you back!"

But a strange calm had settled over him. "I got Cora and Austin back. They'll have each other now."

"Well, good for them," Euri said. "But what about *you*? And growing up? Your life, Jack!"

"I'm not scared of death," he said. "And anyway, everyone already thinks I look dead—"

"You're just depressed," Euri interrupted. "You got rejected and you feel like no one loves you except me."

Jack felt his face grow hot. "That's not true. I chose to send Austin and Cora back. I did the right thing. I was the more loving one."

Euri snorted. "And now you're choosing to stay! That's not being the more loving one, Jack. It's just being a coward."

Jack began to shake. The anger he'd felt when Cora had told him she liked Austin abruptly returned. "What do you know?" he snapped.

"I know how you feel," Euri said quietly. "But you're right about us. It's impossible. You need to keep your promise to me and go."

Jack looked down. He knew Euri was right but the thought of being alone, of having no one, made him hesitate. "Will some girl ever like me?" he whispered.

Euri took his hand and squeezed it. "Some girl already does."

Her hand began to fade into his.

Euri jerked backward. "You're starting to die."

Jack looked down at his hand. If he was already dead, his hand wouldn't be pulsing and fading. He thought about what Viele said—how he had to choose to be alive. He suddenly, desperately wanted to live.

Jack felt a stab of panic. "What am I going to do?"

Euri grabbed Dylan Thomas's pocket watch. "We only have ten minutes. We need to get back to the stream you came in through. The ankle charm only stops me from leaving Bloomingdale, so I can take you almost up to it." She studied his eyes. "You look scared—and still alive. Come on!"

They flew out of the office, Euri leading the way.

"But the Security Alert," Jack said as they flew down the stone corridor and turned into another. "The guards are still going to be there."

"We'll think of something," said Euri.

Jack's feet began to shimmer and fade to the translucent shade of the dead. But even though his feet and hands were now ghostlike, he could feel his heart straining against his chest, full of life and beating fast.

Up ahead was the flooded part of the tunnel. Standing in front of it was a guard.

"I can't go too much closer," Euri whispered. "So we need to get him away from the stream."

She grabbed Jack and shouted to the guard. "I've got the Living Avenger!"

The guard lumbered up to them. "He can't be the . . ." the guard started to say but as he registered Jack's eyes, he lunged forward.

Euri let go of him with a shove. "Run. Go!"

Instinctively, Jack dodged the guard and flew toward the stream. There was no time to thank Euri or say good-bye—no time even to look back. He could hear the guard racing through the air behind him. He touched down just before the flooded part of the tunnel and leaped but instead of sailing forward over the stream, he felt himself being dragged backward by the shoulder. A hand clamped around his arm. The guard was laughing as Jack struggled, trying to free himself.

"Jack!" Euri shouted. He tried to crane his neck in her direction but his face felt strange. The guard was twisting his arm but Jack could barely feel it. The rest of his body was giving out. He struggled to breathe. With his free hand, he dug into his pocket. His fingers seized upon the ghost-repellent pouch and with his last bit of strength, he tore it open and tossed the contents directly into the guard's face.

A horrible smell filled the tunnel. The guard lurched

and dropped Jack. "What the——?" he shouted, clutching his face.

Jack wasn't sure whether he was still alive. His skin felt cold and his teeth were chattering, but he managed to lunge across the stream, falling onto his knees, crawling, and finally rolling, like in a dream, his eyes closed, water seeping into his mouth.

"Good-bye, Jack!" he could hear Euri shout faintly.

His fingernails scraped upon dry ground. Air poured into his lungs. Panting, he struggled back onto his hands and knees and looked back. But the stream had vanished and in its place was a wall of cold, damp stones. He jumped to his feet and ran his fingers against it. They were no longer translucent but Jack wished they were, so he could reach through the wall and grasp Euri's hand. He realized that he had made a terrible mistake—thinking that because it was impossible for him and Euri to be together, he couldn't still love her. "Euri!" he screamed, pounding on the wall.

There was no response.

"Euri!"

His hands began to bleed from the force of his blows.

"I love you!" he shouted.

Jack sank to the floor. His whole body throbbed with exhaustion, and he shut his eyes and sobbed.

Finally, when he was out of tears, he stood up and slowly walked back out of the tunnel.

XXXII | The Invited Guest

It was a gray November Sunday in New York, and outside
the window of Jack's bedroom, snow was beginning to
fall. The sounds of the city dulled—horns grew distant,
shouts softer—and a buzzing stillness echoed through the
apartment. His father was out and it was time to turn on
some lights and finish translating the end of the
Proserpina myth for Latin class. But, instead, Jack watched
the big, thick flakes drift lazily toward the window ledge
and thought about Euri. Now that he was back in the living world, he wanted to see ghosts, and every night he
willed them to appear: a troupe of ballet dancers leaping
from roof to roof, bankers haggling over stock prices as
they flew downtown, bike messengers peddling furiously
through the sky. Jack could control his powers now, but it
didn't matter. He couldn't conjure the one spirit he wanted
to see. Euri was locked away at Bloomingdale.

The doorbell rang. Jack trod in his socks to the foyer,

wondering if Mrs. Finkelstein's cat had escaped her apartment again. But when he opened the door, he saw Cora.

"Hi," she said.

"Hi," Jack murmured. Ever since they had returned from the underworld, he had kept his distance from her. It wasn't that hard, especially since she was hanging out with Austin as much as the Latin Club now. A few times, after Latin class, he had caught her staring at him and sensed she wanted to talk, but he had always hurried off.

After an awkward pause, Jack held open the door and stepped aside. "Want to come in?"

"Thanks," she said, taking off her long black parka.

He pointed to the couch in the living room. Cora sat down and he perched on the opposite arm.

"How's Austin?" he asked. He had meant to sound casual, but he feared the question came out like an accusation.

Cora didn't seem to notice. "Nate's back in college. He's got a new apartment, too. No more hissing cockroaches. Just a few regular ones."

"That's good," said Jack. But he felt disappointed. The end of Nate's cockroach problem was just one more sign that Euri was stuck at Bloomingdale.

Cora's cell phone began to ring. She pulled it out of her pocket and looked down at the number.

"You need to get that?" asked Jack, thankful for the disruption.

Cora shook her head and stuffed the cell phone back into her pocket.

"How's your mom?"

"You know she thinks we all just got locked in the Columbia basement," said Cora with a sly grin. "But you and Euri were right. She did okay. Even without me."

"You did okay, too."

Cora's eyes searched Jack's. "Maybe you could come over some time and meet her?"

"Sure," said Jack.

Cora abruptly stood. And even though he had been wishing the whole time that she hadn't come, Jack suddenly didn't want her to leave. "Do you want a drink or something?" he asked, realizing he probably should have offered her this when she had come in.

She shook her head and put on her coat.

He scrambled to keep her there. "Did you finish tomorrow's Latin homework?"

She turned and put her hand on his arm. "I need to try things out with Austin," she said, "and I can't have you hate me for that."

Jack looked at the floor.

Cora sighed and walked over to the door. She began

to open it, but Jack rushed to stop her. "I gave you Austin back," he said.

"I know. I know exactly what you did."

"I don't hate you." He reached out and touched a lock of her hair. She stood still, like something wild he had caught, a bird briefly resting in his hand. Then footsteps echoed in the hallway, and Cora tucked the lock behind her ear and turned the doorknob. "See you tomorrow," she said.

Jack watched her walk to the elevator, then came back inside and put on his hat and jacket. After he was certain that she was gone, he took the elevator down and began to walk toward the park. The snow had dampened down the city's usual electric spirit. Streetlights flickered and finally switched on.

By the time he reached the park, the snow was sticking to the ground, covering the patchy grass and other blemishes, and turning wood fences and trash cans into lace. The chain-link swings at Specter Playground rocked softly by themselves in the wind. Jack sat down on one of them, swinging slowly. The park began to grow dark—the snow glistening like confetti and glowing under the lamps.

"Hey, there."

Jack turned. Euri was sitting on one of the swings that just moments earlier had seemed to be rocking on its own. He dragged his feet across the snowy ground, slowing himself to a stop. "How did you get out of Bloomingdale?"

"Nice to see you, too," said Euri.

"I mean it's great, but how—"

"They let me out."

Jack must have looked surprised, because she rolled her eyes. "I'm not always an outlaw. I passed my assessment." She stuck her leg in the air. "No more ankle charm. Austin's great-grandfather also put in a good word for me."

Jack thought about Nate and how his cockroach problem had disappeared. "Wait, how long have you been out?"

"Five weeks. I was going to go find you soon."

"Nate—?"

"I stopped haunting him," she said. "I promised Dr. Earle I was done. And I am. But I also told Dr. Earle I'm not ready to move on."

Jack took a deep breath. He couldn't help feeling relieved.

"I'm going to someday, though," she added gently. "Maybe even someday soon."

"I know," he whispered.

"But, Jack?"

"What?"

"I love you, too."

Before he could say anything, she stuck out her tongue. "Let's see who can swing higher! Go!"

Euri didn't even have to pump her legs to make the swing take off. She began to fly back and forth, as high as she could before spinning once completely around the metal bar.

"Show-off," he mumbled.

"Come on!" she shouted.

He thought about Proserpina and the pomegranate—from the Latin *pomum granatum* or *apple of many seeds*—she had tasted. Cora couldn't love him—at least not now. And Euri would leave him someday, as would all the people he loved. For a moment, he felt the temptation to indulge in despair. But Auden was right. There was only one choice. He pumped his legs, closed his eyes, and forced himself to smile. Snowflakes melted against his eyelashes, kissing his face. He suddenly felt loved—not just by the world, but by himself.

Acknowledgments

Jack and Euri continue their journey thanks, in large part, to the following people: Alex Glass, my multitalented agent; Jennifer Besser, my visionary editor; Sarah Self, my enterprising film rep; Lyda Phillips, my talented critique partner; Elaine Milosh, my loving mother and mother's helper; and Julian Barnes, my husband, champion, and best friend.

Many thanks to Team Hyperion, particularly the legendary Angus Killick and tireless Jennifer Corcoran. Heartfelt thanks also go out to Michael Barnes, Michael Cook, Brian Hecht and Doug Gaasterland, Peter Glassman, Franklin Foer and *The New Republic*, Gussie Lewis, Katherine Jentleson, Joe and Anna Mathews, Jeremy Nussbaum, Jennifer Rasmussen, Evelyn Renold, Sally Rieger at the National Cathedral School Latin Department, and Louis Sorkin at the American Museum of Natural History Entomology Section.

Thanks to my family—particularly my generous father and Los Angeles guide, Ken Marsh, and my wonderfully supportive Maine fan club—Donna Barnes and Robert Griffith, Richard Barnes and Sandra Armentrout, and Caitlin, Jared, and Walter Ruthman.

Finally, a special thank-you to the young readers of the Northport–East Northport Public Library Mock Newbery Club for their help critiquing the first chapter and coming up with the title of this book.